Secretly

Book Four in the
Playing for Hearts Series

Debra Kayn

Author of *Conveniently* and *Seductively*

CRIMSON
ROMANCE

F+W Media, Inc.

This edition published by
Crimson Romance
an imprint of F+W Media, Inc.
10151 Carver Road, Suite 200
Blue Ash, Ohio 45242
www.crimsonromance.com

ISBN 10: 1-4405-6653-4
ISBN 13: 978-1-4405-6653-0
eISBN 10: 1-4405-6654-2
eISBN 13: 978-1-4405-6654-7

This one goes to my oldest brother, Doug. He was the football star in the family and because of his sport, I attended every game, practice, camp, and hung out with the team like every little sister wishes she could do. I can still throw a spiral better than most girls, and believe there's no such thing as flag football.

Chapter One

The gravel road crunched under the soles of Angie Swanson's Nike runners. The fierce wind blew off the mountain range and swept her honey-brown hair behind her shoulders. She stopped in the middle of Main Street and squinted into the setting sun, gazing down a barren, straight road.

Of all the places she never imagined herself ending up, it was Deadhorse, Oregon. Worse yet, she always dreamed she'd be working at a major spa, specializing in Swedish massage. Instead, she was the super pumper at her older brother Drew's gas station.

It was, in fact, The Gas Station. Drew couldn't even come up with a better name on the sign, despite her suggestions to glam it up into something more. Angie's Pumps, Octane in Lavender, or even leaning in the direction of hilarity with *Let us pump you up* would've been better than The Gas Station. Drew had rejected all of them for the nondescript, boring name; but that wasn't surprising. He lived in Deadhorse.

Dead. Horse.

She didn't belong here. The slow pace where people only talked about the weather and June Murphy's prized rose bushes outside the post office bored her to tears. To her, they were flowers. Red ones, that looked like any other rose bush in a million other front yards.

She had been born to do something big. Bigger than pumping gas in a deceased animal town where only the wind kept her company.

After spending four years at Washington State University, majoring in Journalism, she'd quickly learned after taking a community class on therapeutic massages that she wanted to change professions. So, she'd left her gopher position at the *Seattle*

Times, and succeeded in landing a posh job at Le Massage. Then, three months ago, after working there almost two years, the spa closed. Unable to afford to keep renting the apartment she shared with her best friend, Jules, she'd taken up Drew's offer to work for him.

Temporarily, of course.

Every day, each longer and more depressing than the last, passed in a blur of mundane information overload, high-strung emotions, and the foolish realization that she should have bought stock in Doritos—for how much they were the main staple of her diet lately. Not to mention last week her father had dropped off her four-year-old half-sister and five-year-old half-brother for two days of fun with big sis while he vacationed with her stepmom. The past three months had been a painful lesson about living in Loserville.

She had to find a job before she lost the rest of her sanity. She glanced down at her sneakers and groaned. Seriously, what kind of place had cow shit in the middle of the road? Obviously there were some animals alive and kicking still around.

She dragged her foot behind her for ten paces, rechecked her sole, and declared it as clean as it'd get. Not that anyone would notice. The smell of gasoline on her clothes overrode *eau de toilette* poo.

Angie would give anything to escape and go back to Seattle. She sighed, gazing up into the sky. Whether it was because she'd hit rock bottom or simply because she wanted something better in her life than living her brother's dream, she'd started scouring the internet and applying for any job she qualified for. And still nobody hired her.

Something had to change soon. She sniffed, and raised her chin. The desire to ride the monorail and go shopping downtown at Nordstrom tempted her each day. But Seattle was twelve hours away. The price of gas alone was too much for her to rent a car to return to the Rose City to visit.

But until circumstances changed, she'd spend her free time pumping gas, washing windshields, and checking tire pressure. She hooked her thumbs in the front pockets of her shorts and walked back toward the gas station, which she'd closed an hour ago. With her brother gone to pick up another project car, she had to work alone. At least he was due back tomorrow, and she'd have someone to talk with during the day.

Distracted by the many things on her wish list, she gave the man leaning against the gas pump a cursory glance and opened her mouth to tell him the gas station was closed when recognition dawned on her. She gasped and covered her mouth.

Tall with huge shoulders, Gary Satchel, the Seattle Seahawks' wide receiver, hijacked her attention. She stood without saying a word, not believing he was here. But it was him. Not just anybody could pull off his size.

His well-worn Levi's, blue and silver Seattle Seahawks football jersey, six foot four inches tall with dark stormy eyes, the two inch scar running the length of his left cheekbone on his handsome face told her everything she needed to know. She raised her gaze and shouted in joy. Her brother's best friend had come to save her.

"Gary," she said on an exhale, launching herself into his arms.

He remained silent, as he was known to do. She closed her eyes, squeezing back the tears of relief at having his famous bear hug wrapping her tightly in his embrace. If there was one person she trusted, besides her brother, it was Gary.

He'd been the solid body she'd clung to during her teenage years when life seemed too cruel to handle alone. Later, he'd become her protector when drunk guys hit on her at the clubs. He always lent her an ear when she needed to talk, and he listened without judgment.

"Sorry to hear about the job, Ang." He inhaled deeply, expanding his chest; she could barely get her arms around him.

She leaned back so she could gaze up at his face. "They picked that asshole Rodden over me to go to Germany to open the new shop. Can you believe that? The guy's rough with his hands and has the bedside manners of a stuck-up prick. The least they could've done is keep the spa open here in Seattle, instead of closing. My clientele alone would've been enough to make it profitable."

He chuckled. "Asshole? Prick?"

"Drew's rubbing off on me. Shop talk—go figure." She shuddered. "What are you doing here?"

She reluctantly stepped away from him and forced her shoulders back. Glad to have someone she knew to talk with, she wasn't going to scare him off by bitching. He gave her hand one more squeeze before letting go.

"I thought I'd stay a couple days, see your brother, and pester you." He motioned for her to walk with him.

"I'm not even going to rise to the bait. I'm seriously lacking in any intelligent conversations. The only things people here talk about are hay prices and how many days until winter." She leaned closer and touched him again to make sure she wasn't hallucinating. "Besides, I get you all to myself. Drew's out on business and won't be home until tomorrow."

"Damn. I'd hoped he'd be around." He pointed to the restored Camaro in the driveway of Drew's house behind the garage. "I wanted to see if he could check the muffler. It's riding rough, and sounds like it's made for the racetrack."

"Ugh. Don't talk cars. That's all I hear about twenty-four/seven. Between the gas station and Drew, I've heard enough to last a lifetime." She walked up the driveway, and noticed his bags lying by the front door. "I am so glad you're here."

"Maybe I should hit the motel." He stopped and put his hand on his car. "I'll come by tomorrow and spend some time with you both."

"Are you crazy?" She grabbed his hand. "I just said this place is boring me to tears. Stay at the house and fill me in on what's happening in the Emerald City. Then I want to pick your brain about places I can send my résumé and—" she swallowed "—afterward, I want to hear what is going on with you."

"Same old thing. Training, meetings, and football." He winked. "What you should do is stay with your friend Jules while you search for a job, so you're in the city and closer to a bigger job market. Nowadays, you almost have to be the first one to apply to get the job and that requires being on location."

"I can't. I already asked her last month if she could do me a favor and let me mooch off her until I find employment. She can't do it. She needs a paying roommate in order to afford the rent." She pouted. "Besides, she's already found a roommate since I left…one with a job."

"Too bad."

She leaned into his arm. "I'm stuck here, unless you're looking to help a family friend out and don't mind having a roommate who can't afford to pay you for a few weeks."

"Absolutely not."

"But, Gary…" She gazed up at him and gave him the saddest, most pathetic look she could muster. "You wouldn't even see or hear me. I'll pay you the back rent once I land a job."

"No."

"I'll clean your house."

"Unlike you, I'm not messy." He laughed. "I don't need a maid."

She glared. "Come on, please?"

"No way." He shook his head. "I've got enough going on with my life. Pre-season practice starts in two weeks."

"Some friend you are. I'd let you stay here if you wanted." She snorted. "What a joke. This place would drive you insane in a week's time."

"Women. Never satisfied." He grunted and thumped the roof of the car as they walked by. "Let's go in the house. I'm beat, and the trip was killer."

Tears came to her eyes. This time she didn't have to fake them. Frustration boiled inside her. She was getting desperate enough to hide in his trunk on the way back to Seattle. Once they arrived, he'd have no choice but to let her stay in his mansion of a condominium.

"Give it up, Ang. The answer's no."

She followed him toward the house. "You don't know what I'm thinking."

"I do." He tugged a strand of her hair and looped it behind her ear. "I've known you too long."

"Whatever." She squeezed past him into the room.

Inside the one-story rambling ranch house, the living room sat in disarray. She'd littered the area with all her belongings, and hadn't found the energy to clean since Drew left a week ago.

There was a pillow and blanket thrown haphazardly on the couch, where she'd curled up to watch a movie in the middle of the night when she couldn't sleep. She hurried over and grabbed her things. Then she threw the contents on a pile of boxes near the fireplace.

"Sorry for the disaster zone." She kept her back turned to Gary, and pushed the box of books out of the middle of the living room. "I'll just move—" she grunted "—everything out to the garage."

"Leave it. I'll help you move everything later. Although, it seems messed up that Drew didn't at least get you situated in a bedroom. Are you sure you haven't killed him, or run him off his own property?" He gripped her shoulders, turned her around, and stared into her eyes. "Tell me you didn't drive him over the edge in three months?"

"No, but I'm taking that as a challenge." She grinned wickedly. "I bet that I can crack you in twelve hours."

"You're probably right." His smile disappeared, and he ran his hand over the top of a box. "So, why is all your stuff in the living room?"

"We moved everything out here when Dad dropped Willie and Desiree off here last week for a couple of days, and they took over my bedroom," she said. "I think my lil bro and sis brought every toy they owned with them."

"You love the chaos." He pointed to the couch. "Sit. Relax."

She plopped down on the couch. "I need excitement in my life that comes from people over the age of twenty-one."

"Well, don't wish too hard. A busy life gets old too." He scratched his chest. "Is there beer in the fridge?"

She shrugged. "I don't know. I haven't looked."

"When did you say Drew left?" He walked across the great room, opened the fridge, and pulled out two bottles of beer.

"Uh, five…six days ago." She rubbed her forehead. "Each miserable day is the same. I might've lost track."

"And you don't know what's in the fridge? What have you been eating?" He twisted the cap off both drinks and passed her one. "Here."

"Thanks." She held the drink in her lap, not lifting it to her mouth. "I eat…stuff."

"Dammit." He stalked back into the kitchen. "Get in here and sit your butt down at the counter."

She stood, walked over to the bar stool, and sat. "Why are you mad?"

"You need to eat wholesome food." He searched the cabinets, and took out a half loaf of bread and a jar of peanut butter. "You had no business jogging if you're not taking care of yourself. You'll make yourself sick—or pass out.

"I've eaten," she mumbled, raising the beer to her mouth.

"What?" He stared at her an extra beat. "Your usual junk?"

"If you have to know, I've eaten two bags of Doritos. Family size." She pointed to the empty bags on the counter. "Nacho flavored, which means there's cheese in it, so I'm getting my calcium."

"That's it?" He shook his head as he plunged a knife into the peanut butter.

"No. I also ate a few of those Little Debbie cupcakes, and the vending machines at The Gas Station have already-made sandwiches. The ham and cheese ones are pretty good." She lifted her chin. "You didn't come back here to complain about my diet, have you?"

"Eat this." He put the sandwich in front of her.

She wrinkled her nose. "I'm not hungry."

"Tough. You need some protein to restore your energy. You're practically dragging your feet." He opened the freezer and dropped a package of frozen meat on the counter. "When you're done with that you'll have a proper dinner."

Gary peeled the butcher paper away, and put a solid chunk of steaks on a plate in the microwave. Angie blinked. "I can't eat all that."

"Honey, only one of those is yours." He turned back around and winked. "It was a long trip, and I'm starving."

She smiled and a short laugh escaped. It was the first real happy sound that had come from her in over a week and surprisingly, it felt good; comforting.

"It's so nice to have you here." She leaned her elbows on the counter. "How long can you stay?"

"Well, here's the thing." He pulled a sack of potatoes out from under the sink. "I've got two days until I'm due for a press conference, so I'm spending the time here. I wish I would've called first, because I was really hoping to catch up with Drew. Between his work and my football, we struggle to get together on a regular basis."

She chewed the last bite of her sandwich, swallowed, and brushed the crumbs from her lips. "At least you'd get to see me almost weekly at the clubs…you know, if I was in Seattle."

"Stop trying to talk me into letting you stay with me." He looked away from her. "It wouldn't be a good idea."

He was hiding something from her. She knew him too well, and he'd been off his game since he'd arrived. More mellow and quiet. His usual easygoing attitude and teasing seemed forced, and every time he looked at her, he quickly looked away. She studied him closely. She'd bet anything he hadn't come to see Drew about fixing his car's muffler. It was something else that had brought him here.

"Oh, no." She cradled her forehead in her hand. "Did you get in trouble?"

He glanced at her. "No. Why would you ask that?"

"I just think something huge brought you to Deadhorse, and your excuse of bringing your car for Drew to look at is lame. It'd take more than that to make me come here." She shrugged. "Something's up, and you can tell me. I won't tell a soul."

"You'll have to wait. I want to tell you when Drew's here." He opened the microwave and removed the defrosted meat. "Besides, I don't want to talk about what brought me here yet when I haven't heard about all the exciting things you've been doing."

"Cruel, Satchel, cruel. My life would kill a man like you." She pushed the broiler pan across the counter. Then she realized whatever he had to share with them must be bothering him more than he was saying, because he'd made the long trip from Seattle to Eastern Oregon.

Three months of bad news was more than a single person should have to put up with, and she'd reached her quota. She watched, fascinated, as Gary stripped the potatoes of their peels. Whatever had happened, she could help. She only had to convince him to let her tag along when he went back home.

Chapter Two

Shut in Drew's bedroom, Gary stood at the window. He stared out into the darkness. No way could he tell Angie the good news without Drew here to run interference. Her impulsive behavior of throwing herself at people and kissing whoever was nearby when she became overcome with happiness called for reinforcements.

Because the news he'd come to share was going to make her dreams come true. He rotated his head, popping his neck. Her good fortune was his punishment.

Being around Angie, alone, was too much for one man to handle. He should've gone with his gut instinct to give her the news over the phone. He'd known exactly how tormenting it would be to see her again. Instead, he'd made up some lie about his muffler, hoping she wouldn't notice that his car purred better than ever.

Angie and Drew were like family. Hell, he and Drew had struck up a friendship their eighth grade year in high school. From day one, they'd been best friends.

Even though he'd grown up just another foster kid in the system, biding his time until he turned eighteen, Drew never treated him any differently. Gary had found a place in the Swanson family. Angie, being a year younger, was the little sister he enjoyed teasing.

Everything changed when she entered high school and he noticed her as a woman, not his best friend's little sister. When she came back from college, he'd gotten the biggest surprise of his life when she threw her arms around him after not seeing him for a year and kissed him hello on the lips. For her, it was just a kiss. To him, it rocked his world.

Since then, he'd only come around when Drew was with her or Angie had a friend with her to act as a buffer. He needed her and

Drew more than he was willing to break them all apart by pissing Drew off and dating his little sister.

His phone beeped. He stepped over to the dresser, retrieved his cell, and read the screen.

U awake?

Leave it to Angie to text him in the middle of the night. He typed, *No.*

Liar.

He moved over and reclined on the bed. *What's wrong?*

Several minutes passed. He wondered if he should go across the hall and talk to her face to face. He closed his eyes for a moment. This was going to be harder than he thought. The last three years, he'd fought his attraction to her. She was like a sister. Hell, she was twenty-five years old, sexier than hell, and if she was any other woman, he'd be in her bed right this minute.

At five foot seven, when other women swayed when they walked, she strutted. And every man in the room noticed. Her breasts were firm and on the larger side, and her ass was tight. The combination was his perfect woman. Strip everything away, and she was smart. She talked about every subject under the sky, and he found himself listening, because she was interesting. He sighed. No, it was her passion. She never did anything without throwing one hundred percent into it.

Can't sleep.

He ran his thumb over the keypad. *Me ne8ter.*

She replied quickly. *LOL Fat thumbs.*

Yeah. Big everything. He groaned and shook his head.

Before he could correct himself, she replied, *TMI.*

Go 2 sleep. He shut off his phone and tossed it to the end of the bed.

He couldn't wait until football started. The sport gave him an excuse to wear off tension, focus on something else besides lusting after Angie. Football was the answer to everything in his experience. It gave him a family, a position in life, a goal. He excelled at the sport and found mentoring from his coaches that kept him straight and focused. Yet, lately, he recognized that he had other needs and wishes. He wanted a relationship. One that stayed all year long and didn't end with the Super Bowl.

The blame for falling for Angie lay on his shoulders. He ran his hands over his face and plopped down on the bed, straight onto his back. Realistically, he should forget about her, move on, and find someone else to love. But his heart didn't know how to give up on a dream.

A soft *tap, tap, tap* came from the door. He rolled off the bed and stood. Worried that Angie had too much stress to handle on her own, he opened the door.

He leaned against the doorframe. "Hey."

In an oversized white T-shirt, she stood in the lighted hallway. Her hair lay in a tangled mess over her shoulders, heavily lidded eyes gazed up at him, and her cheeks were flushed. The sight of her grabbed him by the balls and squeezed. He swept his gaze down her body and swallowed. Twice. Her bare legs, peeking out from below the hem of the shirt, stretched a mile long.

"I can't sleep," she whispered. "Can I sit in here with you?"

Useless to deny her anything, he nodded. He'd damn well run out and get whatever she desired if she asked. And that was the crux of his problem when it came to Drew's sister.

"You'll have to move out of the doorway, big guy." She planted her hand in the middle of his chest and pushed.

He stepped back, snapping out of fantasizing about what would happen the second she stepped into the bedroom. Conscious of standing in his boxers, he moved over and swiped his jeans off the back of the chair in the corner. He grimaced as he pulled the Levi's over his hips and stuffed the erection that he'd received the moment he opened the door inside his pants. *Football. 30 seconds to go. Tied.*

Nothing helped his aroused condition. He glanced over at Angie. Oblivious to what his body and mind were doing, she curled up on his bed and hugged his pillow to her chest. Not taking any chances, he leaned against the windowsill and watched her.

"I hate the nights." She propped her elbow on the mattress and cradled her head in her hand. "All I can think about is having to get up early in the morning to open The Gas Station."

"It's not the worst job a person can have. It pays the bills." He sighed heavily. The news he'd come here with would solve all her problems, but no way could he tell her she was being offered the position as the team massage therapist when she was in his room, in his bed, and the edge of her panties peeked out from below her shirt.

Hell, he wasn't sure how he was going to deal with having her around all the time, much less touching his body. He'd never be able to hide his feelings from her when it was his time to get worked over during practice. Even right now, she tempted him.

White panties. White T-shirt. Tan legs.

He groaned and rubbed the back of his neck. The vision of her laying herself out on the bed for his pleasure was going to kill him.

"At this moment, I can't think of another job I'd hate more." She patted the bed. "Lie down and tell me about Seattle, about our friends, and all the gossip I've missed since I left."

"Not a good idea, Ang."

"Why not?" She scooted over. "It's not like you didn't stay at our house years ago and talk to me late into the night on lots of occasions. You were there all the time."

"With Drew. Not you." He walked over and sat propped against the headboard, as far away from her as he could get.

"That's not true." She squeezed his hand. "We used to all crash in the living room after my mom died. Do you remember?"

He nodded, and then realized she probably couldn't see him sitting in the shadows. "Yeah."

"What do you think is happening at the Metro right now?"

"Women are getting tipsy. Guys are hoping they'll get lucky," he whispered.

"God, I miss it." In the glow of the streetlight coming through the window, she licked her lips. "I keep hoping McGool's Day Spa will call me any day, and I'll have a job. They're the last place that hasn't rejected me, besides the Seahawks. Do you know if the team hired a massage therapist to work alongside the team's physical therapist?"

"Practice for this season hasn't started yet." He pulled his hand away and tugged the sheet over her. "You should get some sleep."

"What are you going to do?" She yawned.

Stay awake and try to figure out how to stop having feelings for you. "Sit here, so you're not alone."

"I could give you a massage…"

"No, thanks."

"It'll put you to sleep," she said.

He snorted. "I doubt it."

"God, I need to get a job. A new job."

"Go to sleep, Ang." He smoothed back the hair on her forehead. "Close your eyes and dream about whatever it is girls dream about."

She pulled her arm out from underneath the blanket. He closed his eyes. If he stopped talking and pretended to rest, maybe she'd go to sleep. He could always go out and lie on the couch if he grew tired enough to shut off his mind.

Her breathing quieted. He rarely saw her anymore. Sure, they ran into each other at the clubs when she lived in Seattle. She'd be with her friends, and he usually ended up leaving because he couldn't stand to see her with other men. Or he'd stay and chase them away. She was full of life, and it killed him to watch her dance and flirt with others while her relationship with him consisted of jokes, slugs to his arm, and reminders of how he was put in her friend category.

She never noticed that his teasing had stopped after his short stint with the Pittsburg Steelers ended and he was traded to his hometown team, the Seattle Seahawks. She'd finished college and with the experiences of an adult, she had a confidence and beauty that grabbed him and never let go. He'd tried to ignore the attraction, so he stayed away, preferring to give her tickets to the games, and making sure Drew was in town and with him when he went over to her apartment.

A half hour later, he opened his eyes. Her hair fanned out across the pillow. He caught one of the loose curls, and rubbed the silky strand between his thumb and finger. Her spirit made everyone around her happy, and to see her depressed and out of her element pained him.

She sighed in contentment. He cupped the top of her head with his hand. His news would change her life. She deserved to have her mind at rest, but he also knew there would be no stopping him from taking her in this bed to celebrate her good news if he told her tonight while they were alone.

She frowned as she rested and squirmed closer. Helpless, he could only be here for her as a friend. He stroked her hair. "Shh."

She jolted awake, peered up at him, and sighed. "Are you sleeping?"

"Yeah." He dropped his chin to his chest. "Go back to sleep. I'll stay here with you."

She laid her head back on the pillow. "I hate sounding whiny. It's just because I'm stressed out. Tomorrow we'll do something fun. 'Kay?"

"You don't—"

"Please." She rolled onto her stomach and looked at him. "We'll go down to Jay's Bar. You'll have to pay because I'm practically broke, but they have a band that comes in. They're not too bad. Nothing like what you can find in Seattle's underground scene, but it'll be fun."

"You'll get your life back, Ang. You just need to give it time."

"That's what Drew says. I hate that answer," she whispered.

"It's the only one I'm giving you." He grinned into the dark. "You're stubborn."

"I'll not only clean your house, I'll chauffeur you to your practices and anywhere else you want to go."

"Give it up."

"I'm serious." She scooted over and laid her head on his lap. "Think about it. No more worries about finding a designated driver when you want to go out and party, food magically showing up in your fridge, and a piece of chocolate on your pillow. It'd be like staying at the ritziest hotel."

"Go to sleep…"

"What if I throw in a personal massage twice a week?" she said, softly.

He closed his eyes. "I'll think about it."

"Yes." She scrambled to her knees and kissed his cheek. "You won't regret it."

"I'm already regretting it, and the answer is no if you don't go to sleep and leave me alone." He growled to prove his point.

She flopped down and curled against him. It took him several minutes to slow his heart rate down from having her pressing against him. Tomorrow, she'd have her news, and begging to live with him would be a moot point. With having her unavailable to him, maybe he could finally move on.

Chapter Three

The bell inside The Gas Station rang, signaling another customer at the pumps. Angie hopped off the stool behind the counter and hurried out the front door. Deadhorse might be a small town, but being close to a major interstate meant there were always customers stopping for gas, and she kept busy.

She leaned over and smiled at the older man driving the Pontiac. "How much can I get you today?"

"Where's Drew?" The man's bushy gray eyebrows met in the middle and he frowned. "Don't tell me he took off on vacation. I was going to have him fix the fender bender my wife received in the parking lot over in Claymont."

"He's coming back today." She glanced behind the car at Gary walking her way. "I'm his sister."

Gary approached the door of the car, laid his hand on her back, and said, "I've got this, Ang. Why don't you go inside? I brought Chinese food back from Claymont and set it on the counter inside. You can eat."

"Thanks." She patted his arm.

Inside the station, the aroma of sweet and sour sauce filled the little room. Her stomach growled. Peeking inside the bag, she pulled out a fortune cookie. Without reading the paper, she popped the cookie in her mouth and tossed the paper on the counter.

The phone rang. She hurried to finish chewing, swallowed, and picked up the receiver. "Hello, you've got The Gas Station. How can I help you?"

"Is Gary Satchel there?"

"Yes, Gary's here. Hang on a minute. He's with a customer." She put the call on hold.

After pushing back the ledger, her notepad, and the order form for the snacks they carried, she grabbed the Germ-X bottle and scrubbed her hands. She sat back down when Gary strolled in.

She pointed in front of her on the counter. "Phone call for you."

"Thanks. I have my home phone number forwarding the calls here today." He picked up the receiver and turned his back. "Satchel here."

Angie spread out some plain white napkins and glanced at him. His skill in the garage surprised her. He'd jumped in on helping the customers, and even changed the oil on a customer's car. He made her day go faster. She enjoyed the companionship and had to admit, she liked to watch his hands and forearms while he worked. The guy was seriously built.

Gary's sense of taking over pumping the gas every time she walked out of the office endeared him to her even more. Although, he still wouldn't share his news with her without Drew here, and she'd tried everything to get him to spill.

"Okay. Thanks for letting me know." He hung up.

She handed him a carton of rice. "Everything okay?"

"Yeah." He ran his hand across the back of his neck. "They've rescheduled the first game, so practice starts a day earlier. I'll have to hit the road early in the morning."

"Oh." She looked at his face. Hope surged in her chest. "That's good, though. You need to get back to life."

"Yeah," he muttered and sat down on the other side of the counter from her.

The wrinkle between his brow, the way he twisted his mouth to chew on the inside of his cheek, and his slumped shoulders told her a different story. She ignored her own selfish reasons for wanting him to go back to Seattle, and split up the fried shrimp. For some reason, Gary wasn't looking forward to going back home.

"Eat up. You don't want to go back and get your ass kicked on the field." She found the plastic silverware at the bottom of the bag and passed him a fork.

Gary stared at the counter. She waved her hand in front of his face. "Did you hear anything I said?"

He pushed her notepad in front of her. "Are these all the places where you've turned in a résumé? Barista? Secretary?"

She picked up the list, and shoved it under the counter. "Don't depress me. Today, it doesn't matter what my future holds. I've promised myself that tomorrow, I'll start all over again with eternal hope of landing a job."

"It matters." He took a bite of rice, chewed, and watched her. "What do you really want to do, Ang? I know you don't want to pump gas, and run a business. That's Drew's thing."

"I want to do massages." She peeked at him. "Why?"

"I don't know. First, you wanted to be a journalist, then a massage therapist, and now I see you reaching for anything to bring in money."

"I know, but—"

"You can barely type. You'd hate being a secretary." He lowered his voice and continued. "I'm wondering if money were no object, what would be your dream?"

"I'll never be in the position where I could dream." She wrinkled her nose. "I need money to survive. Mom's life insurance went mostly to hospital bills. Drew works harder than anyone I know. My dad has his own life with his new family. I need to pay my own way. It's as simple as that. I want to work paycheck to paycheck like every other American."

"Say you won the lottery of all jobs. What would that be?"

She rolled her eyes and shrugged. "That's easy. I'd still give Swedish massages. I'd just be more elite and have an exclusive clientele of the rich and famous. Somewhere that will pump my career, so I'll never have to struggle to find another job."

"You wouldn't hightail it to some exotic island?"

"Nope." She shook her head. "Massage therapy makes me happy. I guess it's not only therapeutic for the customers, it is for me too. I like making others feel better, so they can enjoy life to the fullest."

He stared at her for an extra beat and then nodded. "It's a good dream."

"Why all the questions?" She bit into a shrimp.

"Just curious." He reached over and laid his hand over hers to stop it from fidgeting with her napkin. "I want you to know that whatever happens when Drew gets back, I'll always be around if you need anything."

"You act as if you're leaving me here. Don't do it. Please," she whispered. "I will do anything. I mean *anything*, if you help me out. Just for a couple of weeks, and then you'll be rid of me."

"I'm not talking about you coming to Seattle," he said. "I just want you to know if you need help, financially or emotionally, I'm here for you."

Not understanding where the conversation was heading, she studied him. "You're freaking me out. Is your news bad or good?"

"Good." He nodded. "Really good."

She flipped her hair behind her shoulder. "Since you're waiting for Drew to arrive, it's probably something manly…like you've found a Mustang GTO you want to fix up or some supermodel is warming your bed. I'll clue you in. That kind of news doesn't make a woman squeal with delight."

A car horn honked three times in quick concession. She lifted her gaze and looked out the window. "Finally. Drew's home. Stay here, I'm going to tell him you're here."

She hurried around the counter, flew out the door, and launched herself in her brother's arms. "Guess who's here?"

"Gary. I saw his car in the back." Drew pulled back from her. "Lay off, sis. I was only gone a week."

She grabbed his hand and kept him outside. "I need to talk with you before you see him. It's important."

Drew glanced at her, and then the front door of the gas station. "What happened? More importantly, what did you do?"

"It's great news. I promise." She bounced on her toes. "I almost have Gary convinced to take me back to Seattle with him. I need you to help seal the deal. If I can stay with him, find a job, I can get my own place. He's this—" she pinched her fingers together "—close to agreeing. You can push him the rest of the way. Call in a buddy favor."

"What will you do at his place?" Drew squinted at her.

"I'll be his personal slave. Isn't that great?"

Drew frowned. "How long has he been here?"

"He came yesterday." She waved her hand, changing the subject. "For some reason he wants to talk with you. So, go tell him how awesome it is of him to put me up in his condominium until I find a job."

"Jesus, sis. Lay off, you're fine staying here until something works out…and things will work out, just give it time." He rubbed the back of his neck. "Do me a favor and go get us all a beer. I want to talk to Gary alone for a minute."

"Yeah, okay." She leaned toward him. "Please, do this for me."

He motioned with his chin. "Go on. I'll see what's going on with him."

She jogged behind The Gas Station to the house, and hurried inside to grab three bottles of beer. On her return trip, she slowed to a walk. She'd give Drew time to work on pulling a favor on her behalf. She skipped in step, smiling hugely, giddy with the thought of leaving in the morning.

Slipping inside the garage, she looked at Drew and Gary. "Well? Did I miss the news?"

Her brother's head dipped and he tried to hide a smile. She gazed over at Gary. He closed his eyes briefly and nodded to her. She handed out the beer, setting hers on the counter for later.

"So…" She held her hands out, palms up, and looked around expectantly. "What's the news?

Drew cleared his throat. "I think this is Gary's news to share."

"Are you sure?" Gary grinned. "I thought you'd want to do it."

"We could flip a coin." Drew shrugged. "Or we could wait until later. It's not closing time, and that way we could celebrate tonight."

"That's a good idea, bro." Gary stretched his back. "It's been a long day. Pumping gas is hard work."

"Okay, knock it off." She crossed her arms, tapped her foot, and pinned Gary to the spot. "I know what you two are doing. Just tell me."

He stepped forward and put his hands on her shoulders. "I want you to think long and hard over what I'm going to tell you. You don't have to do it. It might not even be something that you'll enjoy."

She slugged his arm. "Unless you tell me, how will I know what you're talking about?"

"Fine. I'll tell you." He laughed. "I talked to Mr. Canbridge, human resources manager for the Seahawks…"

"Oh, God." Her heart raced and she grabbed on to his arm. "Go on."

"I ran into him while I was filling out new paperwork, and I asked if he'd found anyone to work beside John Stevens," he said.

"That's the physical therapist who I had the interview with right before I left Seattle," she said, a sinking feeling settling in her stomach.

"Yeah…" His eyes softened and he patted her shoulder. "Turns out, I know the woman who applied for the job as the new massage specialist."

"Oh." She swallowed, trying hard not to let her disappointment show. When she'd applied, she knew it was a long shot. With a short past work history on her résumé, she was afraid the Seahawks would pass her over for someone with more experience. She couldn't fault them. Working with a professional football team was a cushier job than the others she'd been applying for.

"Anyways…" Gary grinned over her head at Drew. "The new gal starts in two days, and since Canbridge knew I was coming out here to visit Drew, I asked him if I could give you the news myself. He agreed."

"Well, thanks…I guess." She wrinkled her nose. "I'll make sure I check them off my list. Although, honestly, dude, I would've preferred to get the customary rejection email notifying me that the position was filled and thanks for applying."

"You're not listening, Ang." He laughed. "*You* start the job in two days. I'm taking you back to Seattle with me."

"Get out!" She smacked her hand over her mouth.

"They hired you. You'll have to wait until you meet with John Stevens to get all the details, but as of Monday, you'll be employed full time by the Seattle Sea—"

She jumped and wrapped her arms around his neck. In her excitement, she kissed him full on the mouth. She pulled back, her legs around his waist, her arms around his neck. "Thank you! That's the best news ever. You've totally saved my life."

She wiggled off him, and threw herself at her brother. After she kissed her brother's cheek, she sank her fingers into her hair and gazed around the room. "I have so much to do. I need to pack, and find an apartment. Oh, I wonder if I can find one close to work." She squealed. "No matter, I'll be flying with the team, too, and I have my car still in storage and I can figure out everything later. This is going to be great. I can't wait."

"Slow down." Drew laughed. "We'll help you pack a few bags and later I'll have all your boxes delivered for you. For right now, I asked Gary to let you stay at his place, until you can get your own apartment. Congratulations, sis. This is huge."

She smiled, launching herself at Gary again. "Thank you! This is a dream."

Wrapped up in his thick arms, cushioned against his chest, she closed her eyes to keep the happiness from reducing her to tears. This was perfect.

Chapter Four

I'm an asshole.

Gary closed the door of his condominium. He threw his bags on the hardwood floor beside Angie's luggage that he'd brought in moments ago, while Angie ran for the bathroom the moment they arrived back at his place in Seattle.

What was he thinking? He knew Drew would ask him to let Angie stay with him. He knew he'd say yes. He knew that was the reason why he'd personally driven to Deadhorse to give Angie the news.

He was in deep shit.

Every fantasy he had of Angie took place in his house, having her in his bed. He gazed across the main room into the kitchen and groaned. And on the table and floor. Hell, his mind took him out of the condo to the stadium, Metro, and the fucking Space Needle.

Angie strolled into the living room and plopped down on the couch. "I don't know whether it's being back in Seattle or the fact that I no longer have to pee, but it feels wonderful to be back in the Emerald City."

"You drank three super-sized Cokes between Portland and Seattle. I imagine you're hyped up on sugar." Gary walked across the room and opened the drapes, casting light into the open spaced area that housed his living room, kitchen, and dining room. "I'll put your things in the spare bedroom."

"I'll help." She jumped up and took the heaviest bag.

He grabbed the handle from her and shook his head. "You can grab the small one."

She rolled her eyes, but refrained from arguing. He marched toward the hallway, and then turned left into the room that would be hers for the next however long it would take her to save up enough money to rent her own place. When he turned around, she remained in the doorway gazing across the hall into his bedroom.

He followed her gaze, and couldn't figure out what grabbed her attention. It was a typical bedroom, one he only slept in. "What's wrong?"

"Please tell me I can sleep in your bed when you're gone," she said.

He looked over her head and smiled. The massive, plush bed had been a present to himself at the end of last season. Custom made, the mattress would fit six normal-sized people or one of him and Angie. It had taken the wood craftsman two months to design the headboard and the four posts that capped each corner.

"Stay out of my bed," he said.

She turned and lifted her chin. "You do realize if you're not here, you won't know where I sleep."

He grunted. "I'll know."

"I don't think you will." She grinned. "I'm sneaky like that."

He leaned toward her. "I'll know."

"How?" She tilted her head.

He inhaled deeply, and even a foot away, he could smell the warm scent coming from her that reminded him of a tropical scented shirt coming straight out of the dryer. "I can smell you."

A rude noise came from her throat and her mouth opened. He chuckled and walked around her. That came out totally wrong, but he needed her to keep her distance. As long as she thought he was turned off by her smell, she'd never find out that he got a hard-on whenever she was in the same room.

She followed him into the kitchen. "What do you mean, I stink?"

He pulled out a water bottle. "Didn't say it was a bad thing." He eyed her. "Just different than me."

She glared, huffed, and left the room. He leaned against the counter. The sooner she earned enough to find her own place to live, the quicker his life would go back to normal. He had bigger things to worry about, like practice starting next week and figuring out how in the hell he was going to keep his distance from Angie for the next seven days.

His phone vibrated. He pulled it out of his pocket. Angie.

FYI, I'm taking a shower.

He closed his eyes for a beat, then typed, *U don't stink.*

She replied, *Dumbass.*

He gazed down the hall. He should apologize. Instead, he changed the subject. *I'll order pizza.*

He waited, and finally she answered. *Pepperoni* :)

Growling, because that was easier than laughing, he pushed a few buttons and called Petro's Pizza. Then he headed to his room to take a quick shower. A cold shower.

Twenty minutes later, he pulled a T-shirt over his head and answered the door. He paid the deliveryman, and carried the cardboard box into the living room. Angie walked into the room with her wet hair hanging around her shoulders, her cheeks flushed, and looking beautiful. He stopped a few feet from the couch and his appetite for food disappeared.

"Hey," he said.

"If you tell me I stink, I'm calling you a liar." She removed the pizza box from his grasp and set it down on the coffee table.

"Ang…" He sat down beside her. "You don't stink, honey."

She grabbed a slice of pizza and lifted it toward her mouth. "Of course not, I took a shower."

Her lips opened and she slowly took the pointed side of the triangle into her mouth. He watched as her eyes closed and she chewed, ending the erotic display with licking her lips clean. He cleaned his throat and looked away. "You smell like a woman."

Angie elbowed him and covered her mouth until she was done chewing her next bite. "That's…wow, too much information and—"

"It's good." He picked up a slice of pizza and eyed the topping. "Better than good. That's why I don't want you in my bed."

"Oh, you can suck up." Angie laughed. "Too late, and it doesn't matter what you want or don't want. I'm going to sleep in your bed, because when you're not here there's no one to stop me. It's a new house rule."

He shoved the rest of the piece of pizza in his mouth. The direction the conversation headed scared him. The next thing she'd ask for would be to share his bed while he was home. He knew her. She hated to be alone. She talked a lot, and that required having someone around to listen to her.

This roommate status was going to kill him.

"Maybe you should call Jules and see if she wants to hang out. Not here at the condo, but maybe someone else. You could go see a movie or the mall." He walked over to the open kitchen and grabbed a stack of paper napkins. Returning to the couch, he glanced at Angie. "I'm sure you have a lot of things you want to do, and I'll be busy."

"I thought practice didn't start until next week." She accepted the napkin from him and wiped her hands. "When I called and received my schedule before we left Deadhorse, you said on Monday you'd be going to the field too."

He nodded. "Yeah…so, you'll want to get all your running around done this week. You might as well use all the free time to catch up on everything you missed doing while you stayed with Drew."

"Good idea." She pulled her bare feet up on the couch and leaned back. "Hey, how about we go out on Saturday. I'll call Jules. We'll take you out, and I'll even buy your drinks. I have enough money to splurge for one night."

He finished polishing off his fourth piece of pizza. "I don't think so."

"Why not?"

"Because." He wadded up his napkin. "You're Drew's sister."

He offered her another slice. She shook her head, turning any more pizza down. He closed the box and carried it to the refrigerator. There was no way in hell he'd go out with her, as friends, roommates, or as a family acquaintance. He was walking on ice, and having Jules present wasn't a strong enough buffer to keep him from doing something stupid.

"Fine. Be a boring dude who only lives for football and his big ass beautiful bed." She leaned forward until her hair hung clear to the floor and her head was upside down. "Someday you're going to wake up and realize life passed you by and that you really should've spent more time with me while you could. I won't always be around to entertain you, you know."

He stared at her, not following the conversation. She was right here. Where was she going, except to her own apartment when she earned enough money?

"Where do you think you're going?" He leaned against the counter, keeping his distance, and talked to her from the kitchen.

She turned her head, flipped her hair, and straightened. "I'm just saying, you never know what will happen tomorrow, next week, or in a year. I might live in Japan making a million dollars next year or I could get in a car crash and—"

"Okay, I'll go." He pushed off the counter and rubbed his tightening chest. "Don't say shit like that. Shit. Make it one of your house rules if you have to, just don't go there."

The thought of losing her from his life hurt. He never had her to himself, but to think she believed her life could end at any moment was too morbid for him to think about.

"It's true. Nobody knows what will happen in the future." She studied him, frowning. "Haven't you ever thought about how cruel life is sometimes?"

"I don't think about it," he muttered.

"Sorry." She sighed. "But I'm glad you'll go out with me. We'll have fun."

"Yeah." He crossed his chest with his arm and slapped a hand on his opposite shoulder, rotating the joint. "I'm going to go out for a jog and wear off some of this pizza."

"Okay." She reached for the television remote.

He walked to his room and put on his shorts, socks, and shoes. Jogging was the last thing he wanted to do, but he had to get out of here. Angie was messing with his head. He'd had no idea she thought about what could happen to her. Yet, it made sense. She'd lost her mom as a teenager. He'd seen her struggle with the loss, and fear death visiting Drew next.

She'd been old enough to understand how cancer took her mom's life, and too young to deal with losing the only parent who brought her security. It was understandable that she feared something else could happen to upset her life. He grimaced. Back when her mom died, he'd sat with her for hours, telling her nothing was going to happen. She'd believed him, but he'd pulled away from her.

Dressed to go out and exercise, he left the bedroom. In the living room music played. He glanced over to wave at Angie, and stubbed the toe of his sneaker on the floor at the sight of her.

She danced in front of the window with her back turned toward him, her arms above her head, her ass swaying, her hair flowing. He hardened, and all he could do was stand there like a fucking loser while ogling her.

He moved toward her and was halfway across the room when she turned. Instead of surprise at finding him there, she smiled and continued dancing.

"I love this song," she said, continuing to dance her way closer.

He hitched his thumb over his shoulder. "I'm leaving."

She nodded and gave him a thumbs up. He laughed. Shit, she was funny.

He walked out of the condominium and started out at a slow jog; until he lost his erection, he wasn't going to make it out of the parking lot. He'd worried about her talk of death for nothing. She went from deep life questions to fluttering around his living room without a care.

He only had to survive six days, twelve hours, and too many more minutes with her and then he'd be back to playing football and taking his frustrations out on the field.

Chapter Five

Four nights later, Angie still couldn't sleep for more than two hours at a time. Every single night since moving in with Gary, she'd fought with the blankets, finding herself restless and frustrated. She flipped over her pillow, hoping the cool side would calm her enough to go to sleep.

When was the last night she'd slept at least six hours? Not that she ever had an easy time sleeping since before getting the news that her mom had breast cancer.

She snuggled under the covers on a sigh. That wasn't true. The last night she stayed at her brother's house and slept in bed with Gary, she'd slept like a baby.

She hated the nights. In the quiet and darkness, she could never forget waking up and finding out her mom had passed away. Growing up, her brother would take pity on her and stay up talking through the night. Even Gary had indulged her need to stay awake, and would sometimes keep her company before he'd left for college. But as soon as she closed her eyes, she'd remember.

She tossed back the covers and grabbed her phone off the nightstand. Putting thumbs to the keyboard, she typed. *U awake?*

Several minutes later, she stretched out to put down the phone, thinking he was asleep, when the cell vibrated in her hand.

No.

Warmth curled inside her. *Can I ask U something?*

Go to sleep, A.

Please?

She waited. If he wasn't asleep, what was he doing? She looked at the closed door to her room. He was right on the other side of the hall, but no noise came to her. Maybe he was restless too.

Her phone buzzed. She peered down and read. *What?*

She sucked in her bottom lip. If she texted him, what would she say? She was scared to sleep at his condo? She has never been able to rest comfortably alone? She groaned and put the phone on the table, swung her legs off the bed, and sat on the edge. He'd think she was a baby, and he already seemed to view her only as Drew's little sister, as if she never grew up and became an adult.

Her wanting to sleep in his bed with him was more than being afraid. There was something about him that gave her comfort. He had the best hugs of anyone she knew. It probably had to do with his size, since he was also bigger than anyone she knew. A defensive end who ate a balanced meal and kept himself in rock-hard shape: perfect for cuddling. When his hand laid on her back or he stroked her hair, she knew nothing would happen to her.

But needing him came from deep inside of her. He was comfortable, and no matter what, he'd always been around. She depended on him. Being with him brought normalcy back into her life, like it used to be before her mom passed away and Drew moved on with his own life.

She stood and walked to the door before she could change her mind. Texting him was a bad idea. What she wanted from him could only be said in person, so he couldn't turn her down.

She crossed the hallway and knocked. He opened the door and leaned against the doorframe. She settled on the large expanse of chest at eye level.

"You should be in bed," he whispered.

"I know, but…" She raised her gaze and stepped in front of him. "Can I sleep with you, please?"

He tilted his head and gazed at the ceiling. "Take the side of the bed closest to the window. Don't hog the blankets."

She threw her arms around his waist and buried her head into his chest. "Thank you. I'll pay you back. Tomorrow, I'll make cookies…or buy some at the Fifth Street bakery."

Then she scurried around him and dove onto the bed, crawling across the massive surface before he could change his mind. Following his orders, she hugged the edge of the bed.

When Gary stretched out on the other side, she couldn't even feel the indentation from his body, the bed was that large. She slid her arm under the pillow and snuggled on her side facing him. The sheets already warmed, she knew she'd taken his spot. Her stomach flip-flopped and she gazed at Gary in the dark. She couldn't see his face, only his large outline. He hadn't gotten under the covers, but lay on top of the comforter on his back.

He slept in his boxers. She puffed up her cheeks and let the air out. A solid rock of a man, he really was beautiful. She lowered her eyelids, peeking out between the lashes.

They'd grown apart over the last few years. She really knew nothing about his private life anymore. Since she'd been here, no girlfriend had stormed the condo demanding to know why he had a woman staying with him. Of course, she kept up with any news about his career and how he was doing through Drew, but she had no idea if he even had someone special in his life.

"Do you have a girlfriend?" she whispered.

His head turned toward her. "What kind of stupid ass question is that?"

"I value living." She pulled her arm out from under the blanket and rested it on the bed. "I should know if you have anyone in your life that's going to kick my ass for staying with you."

"You're Drew's little sister. Why would it matter?" he asked.

She laughed into her pillow. "Okay, obviously the answer is no, you don't have a girl in your life. Trust me, women don't think like men. If you had a girlfriend, she wouldn't like me being here, even if we're family friends. Women are territorial. She'd see me as a threat, and wouldn't trust you not to sleep in your own room."

"Moot point, since you're in my room," he muttered.

"Huh." She inhaled deeply. "But we wouldn't tell her that…I mean, if you had a girlfriend that you were into. Not that it would be fair to her to keep secrets—that's wrong, don't ever do that—but it'd be easier for both of us if we just act normal. So, I won't tell anyone, not that I was going to. Like, really, who would I tell? Drew? That'd be messed up, plus he wouldn't care. Jules might like to know if I was sleeping with you, but she'd go all whacked and assume we're really—"

"No one will bother you. Football season is starting and I don't date when I'm playing," he muttered. "Now go to sleep."

Confused, she wondered if he was cranky over not having a woman around him or if abstinence really did drive a man mad after awhile. She rolled onto her back and stared at the ceiling. Every time she'd run into him in the city, he was either with a couple of his friends who were also professional athletes or with Drew. There were always girls around, but nobody that stood out as someone he was serious about.

For that matter, she hadn't been that serious with anyone either. Sure, she dated a lot and she had an okay sex life, but she'd never quite found Mr. Right. Not that she'd looked too hard—she was too busy growing up and trying to establish herself.

Feeling self-centered around her own problems, she decided from here until her first paycheck arrived and she could move out, she'd catch up more on Gary's life. Always a loner, even in a crowd, he deserved all the good things that happened in his life. He had no one. His birth mother had given him up to the state when he was six years old, and he'd never connected with any of his numerous foster parents. That was why Gary spent most of his time with Drew growing up. It was hard to feel content at home when his guardians put him on an if-we-have-time-for-you list; which they never did. As soon as he turned eighteen, he was on his own.

That would all change now that she was back in town. She'd support him, and because of her new job, she'd also be at every game to cheer him on. A quiver of excitement went through her.

She couldn't believe she was the massage therapist for the Seattle Seahawks. Could life get any better?

No way would she ever have thought she'd get the job, but Gary had encouraged her over the phone to try for the spot when she'd moved to Deadhorse. She owed him for giving her the tip about the job.

In the next second, her thoughts shifted and she worried. What if she couldn't do the job? She had experience, and she was damn good. But the boys on the team were big. They had muscles where normal people didn't, and their bodies were their tool to earning a nice living.

Gary's body was perfect.

She rolled to her side and stared at him in the dark. Better than perfect.

On the car trip back from Deadhorse, she'd noticed his thighs and forearms. How could she not, when there was nothing to view out the window? The way he handled the car fascinated her. He made moving look graceful and natural. She warmed and threw the blanket off her upper body. She hid her curiosity from him, but she wondered what he was like as a boyfriend.

All she'd ever experienced were his great hugs. Once in a while, she'd kiss him to show him thanks for helping her out, but he always pulled away or held her shoulders, distancing himself. Just one time, she'd like to experience his full lips for more than two seconds.

She leaned up on her elbow and studied Gary's form. His breathing came deep and even. Getting up on her hands and knees, she carefully crawled closer. When she was beside him, she slowly lay down. With her head on his chest, she let herself relax, content to be near him.

She closed her eyes, aware of Gary's warmth, the rhythm of his breathing lulling her to sleep. Promising herself she'd move back to her side of the bed before he woke in the morning, she settled down for the night.

Chapter Six

A car horn outside woke Gary. He blinked sleep away, aware of a pleasant warm weight lying atop him. Lifting his head off the pillow, he gazed down his body.

Angie lay between his sprawled legs, her head cushioned on his stomach, the heat of her body pressed against the biggest hard-on he'd ever had. His head hit the pillow and he stared up at the ceiling. *12 to 11 in the fourth quarter with twenty seconds remaining. The running back has the ball. I stand between the opponent and the end zone.*

He groaned. Quoting football plays wasn't going to work this morning. Angie was soft and pliable. He was hard, and he wanted her. There was no way he could extract himself out from under her without waking her up. There was also no way she would miss his erection when she became conscious. He lifted his hand, hovering his palm over her hair. He curled his fingers into a fist and dropped his arm onto the bed without touching her. *Shit.*

Being Drew's friend sucked. He should call him up and tell him he was never going to see or talk with him again. Their friendship was over, because Gary was going to have sex with Drew's little sister. He'd…

Fuck, I sound like I'm breaking up with Drew.

Angie squirmed. He flinched, bracing for the pain when her shoulder settled in his crotch. Only more pleasure came his way, and his heart threatened to burst out of his chest. The room compressed in on him and all he could feel was the pressure of Angie on him.

"Gar…?" She rubbed her cheek along the bare skin of his abdomen and opened her eyes.

The moment she spotted him, her gaze warmed and she sighed heavily, perfectly content to cuddle against him. "Morning."

He cleared his throat, buying time to unstick his tongue from the roof of his mouth. "Hey."

"What time is it?" She stifled a yawn.

Her mouth opened and then her warm breath tickled his skin. His cock responded, his balls tightened, and he groaned as he lunged, hauling her off him in one swoop. She bounced on the mattress, and he jumped out of bed, keeping his back toward her.

"Time to get up. I'm going for a jog." He strode across the room and escaped into the bathroom.

One cold shower later, he peeked out into the bedroom and breathed in relief to find the room empty. He quickly pulled a pair of sweats and a T-shirt out of the drawer, and dressed. For the next hour, he'd have an excuse to stay away from her.

The cool morning Seattle air, the separation of mind and body, and physical exertion would get Angie off his mind.

He exited the bedroom at the same time Angie walked out of her bedroom. He stopped, sweeping his gaze over her. A bad feeling came over him.

She tightened her ponytail. "Ready?"

"For what?" He crossed his arms.

She wore a skimpy pair of shorts, an oversized sweatshirt, and a pair of running shoes. Dread mixed with curiosity raged against each other inside of him. He'd really love to see her running in those shorts, but there was no way in hell he'd let her go jogging with him.

"I'll partner with you this morning. I haven't exercised in over a week." She patted his chest. "It'll be good for me."

"If I told you I like to run alone, would you stay home and leave me in peace?" He followed her down the hall.

"Fine." She pushed up her sleeves and glanced over her shoulder. "I'll jog behind you. You won't even know I'm there. If you think you can lose me, feel free to try. I know my way around and will run my own route."

"I don't need a personal trainer," he said.

"Not trying to be one." She shrugged. "It's just if you want to be alone, you better be faster than me. That's all."

"You think you can out run me?" He laughed. "Really?"

She arched her brows and pursed her lips. "Whatever, big bad football star."

He shook his head in amusement, but his humor fled at the weary gaze that darted away and stared at the floor.

She grabbed the door handle. He planted his hand over her shoulder on the door, and stopped her from going out. This close, he inhaled the vanilla scent he was getting used to recognizing as her.

He sighed. "What are you doing, honey?"

She turned and put her back to the door and looked up at him. "I want to be with you."

"I'm not stopping at the nearest convenience store for donuts and chips." He studied her.

She scoffed. "Just because you have a problem with all the junk food I eat doesn't mean I don't try to balance the food groups with exercise."

He remained silent. She was avoiding his question. Twice now she'd crawled into his bed, and he wanted to know why. Now she wanted to hang with him while he exercised. No, something was going on in her head, and he wanted to know what she was thinking.

"You'll jog in front of me, and when you get tired, we'll stop." He straightened. Two could play at this game, and if she wanted to prove a point, he sure in the hell could enjoy the scenery of her jogging in her tight blue shorts while she figured out what she was doing.

"Fine." She swooped through the door and called over her shoulder, "Don't let the dust choke you."

Cute. He let her jog ahead fifty feet, and then kicked up the pace to a fast walk. He'd wait her out. She'd tire and he'd take her back to the apartment. Maybe he'd slip into the workout room at the community center at the condominium later instead of worrying about getting his three miles in.

Angie rounded the corner and for a second, Gary lost sight of her. He burst forward at a jog, gaining ground. He should catch up with her on the next corner.

Three blocks later, Angie still remained ahead of him by a good twenty-five feet. He pumped his arms, finding his pace. Obviously she was in better shape than he'd realized. But he wasn't worried. With his longer legs, he'd eventually catch her.

He relaxed and enjoyed the jog. His gaze stayed on her, following her lead as he grew closer. Preferring to go out in the morning alone, he'd never noticed the benefits of a run with someone else.

He pushed her. The pace helped his heart rate, and the scenery was spectacular.

Angie's ponytail swayed from side to side. She stayed focus on her path, her shoulders straight, her elbows bent. His gaze lowered. Her ass tight, round, and—

His body pitched forward. He stumbled to keep his feet under him, and lost the battle. He dove for the grassy area to the left of the sidewalk to avoid the concrete and rolled. A grunt expelled from his lungs on impact, and he lay on his back, looking up at the sky.

A single raindrop hit his chin. He peered up into the gray cloud rolling across the sky. Damn Seattle weather.

Angie's face blocked his view of the clouds. "Are you okay?"

He hoisted himself to his feet, groaning. Angie brushed off a few strands of grass from the front of his shirt. This close to her, he could see the rise and fall of her breasts as she caught her breath. His already racing heart was doing overtime.

"Yeah." He stepped away, testing his knees. "I make tackles for a living. I'm used to crashing."

Excuses. He sounded like an asshole. What was he going to say? He'd tripped on a crack in the sidewalk. A fucking crack.

"If you're sure." Angie frowned, studying him. "Are you feeling all right? You look kind of weird. Your face is flushed and you're sweating."

The rain picked up. He motioned his chin. "Let's head back. I don't feel like jogging in the rain."

"Okay." She stayed beside him, taking two strides for each one of his.

He had to give her credit. "You run often?"

She glanced over at him without slowing her pace. "Every other day. I've only worked up to four miles, but I enjoy being outside and clearing my head. Gives me time to think."

"Yeah, I get that." He turned the corner. The Angie he knew back when she was a teenager would never have taken up any form of exercise. The fact that she was on a dedicated running program impressed him. Not that she needed the exercise, but that she enjoyed running alone. He always pictured her around a group of girls, or more content to hang out at a gym.

"You might think about where you're going to live when you get enough money for a deposit. It'll have to be in a nice area, so you're safe and can continue jogging. You'll probably want to stay away from the downtown area, because of the steep street levels." He pointed across the road. "About six blocks over there are new apartments. Half are done, and the rest are still being built. You'll probably have a year of construction headaches, but once it's over it'll be a nice area."

"How much?" She slowed to a walk.

He followed her lead, and joined her as they cooled down at the entrance to the gated area of the condominiums. "Not sure, but I could call a guy I know. He's a realtor. Does property management for most of the area around here."

"Okay. Thanks." She wiped her forearm across her forehead. "I'd like to stay around fifteen hundred a month, if I can."

He laughed. "You won't find anything in that price range around this area. You're used to having a roommate…you might want to ask around and see if you have a girlfriend who is looking to double up."

She pursed her lips. He studied the stubborn tilt of her chin and furrowed brow.

"What? You don't like the idea of sharing a place?"

"I was thinking I'd live alone." She shrugged, following him up the driveway to his place. "I loved living with Jules, but the constant go-go-go of being around friends, especially girls, gets old."

He laid his arm across her shoulder and squeezed. "Little Angie is growing up."

"Maybe." She grinned up at him. "Nah."

He dropped his arm and opened the door. "You'll probably have to go further out of town to find rent at the price you want. Maybe an older home or studio, instead of a gated apartment."

"I was thinking of a studio off the pier. I know the price is higher and I can crunch some numbers if I have to, but I like the atmosphere. It's artsy, relaxing, and I'm by the water," she said.

"Hell no." He shook his head. "It's not safe. You'd never be able to go out alone, much less take a run when you wanted."

"Why not?" She laughed. "I grew up in Seattle. I know where everything is, and have never had any problems. I've gone downtown many times by myself."

"You're not moving downtown." He swept off his shirt. "I'll show you why. Go change clothes, and I'll drive you down to the pier. We'll make a day of it, and I'll show you what you're missing when you're not paying attention."

"I know the area, Gary." She pulled the band from her ponytail and shook her head. "But fine, I'll take you up on your offer. Maybe I'll find a wonderful place and they'll take a security deposit for the first and last month's rent if I sign on to give them the rest in two weeks."

"If you find something you can't live without, I can loan you the money," he said.

"Really?" She smiled.

"But not in that area." He turned and walked down the hall. "We'll find you a nice place…one with a security alarm."

She laughed, and he shut the door. Standing in his bedroom, he knew taking her out on the town was a bad idea. She was a beautiful woman, and it wasn't safe for her to live alone… anywhere. If he were Drew, he'd never allow her to live by herself.

But if she had her heart set on a place, he'd help her out. As a friend or brother would do. He stripped off his clothes and walked into the bathroom. Maybe he could hire a security firm to beef up her new place, and that way he could sleep at night without worrying about her being all alone.

Chapter Seven

The third place Angie dragged Gary to on their apartment hunting foray along the Pike was a studio flat above a tattoo parlor across from the wharf. She climbed the steep stairs behind the building manager up to the advertised room, and glanced behind her at Gary. She winked, feeling good about the place.

At first glance, the place was perfect. No pedestrians stood loitering outside on the sidewalk, and the stairwell was quiet enough she could hear every creak of the old boards under her shoes. If it weren't for the row of cars parked outside along the street, she'd think the tattoo business up and closed shop, because the silence coming from underneath them was heaven.

"Right through here." Matt, the manager, stepped back and opened the door for them. "I think you'll enjoy all the natural light coming through the windows. A rare commodity in Seattle."

She smiled and slipped inside, gasping at the sight.

Floor to ceiling windows on the west side of the building overlooked the water. She hurried across the room and peered down into the street. The location was near perfect for what she was looking for.

A ferry docked off the pier fit the local flavor scenery she came to expect from Seattle. People of all lifestyles milled up and down the sidewalk on the other side of the street, shopping or enjoying the overcast day. Most of all, she sensed what she was looking for: here, she could observe life without life invading her space. With her busy work schedule, her days off would stimulate but relax her as she enjoyed her little slice of privacy.

"Let's get out of here, Ang," Gary muttered.

"What?" She whirled around and stared at him in confusion. "It's perfect. The location, the price—did you see the six panel wood door? It's absolutely charming and old world."

He shook his head. "No, it's not. Let's go."

"I want to put an offer down." She grabbed Gary's arm. "Please. It's everything I was looking for. I'll be close to everything. It'll take no time to drive to my job or take a taxi if I don't want to fight traffic. I can walk to go shopping. If I go jogging, I can run parallel to the water and won't have to deal with the steep side streets. And the price is right. I'll save the extra two hundred dollars, because parking comes free with the rent. I could even take on a few clients and give massages out of the—"

"No." He leaned in and said, "We're leaving. Now. Don't argue with me."

He grasped her hand and nodded at Matt as he pulled her out of the studio, down the stairs, and along the sidewalk. At the end of the block, she snapped out of letting him get his way, and planted her feet.

"Why not?" She held up both her arms. "Give me one freaking reason why you jumped into my business and tore out of the building? You're embarrassing me! I'm trying to make a good impression on the landlord, not that I'm rude or my friends are—"

"Look." He laid his hands on her shoulders, turned her around, and whispered in her ear. "See the sign for the tattoo parlor?"

A white rectangle sign with the words *Body Stainers* written in black hung from the building and out over the sidewalk. She nodded. "So?"

"Look in the right bottom corner. Do you see the four point crown?" he asked.

"Yeah, but what does this have to do with me and wanting that studio?" She turned around. "It doesn't excuse you being an overprotective bully. God, you act just like Drew."

"That's a business owned by the Los Gatos. Have you heard of them before?"

"Shit..." she mumbled. She'd heard of them, read of their exploits, and viewed their handy work around town when someone tried to encroach on their territory. They were a gang that other gangs stayed far away from. Real bad guys you didn't want to mess with.

"Yeah." He inhaled deeply and blew out his cheeks. "What you don't see right in front of you are the signs that they run this district…not all of the businesses in the area, but enough that their presence is felt and respected if you want to stay in business. It's not a safe enough place for you to live, especially in a building that is run by people who don't care that a woman alone could be walking into trouble, living right above trouble, thrives on getting in trouble because she's too curious for her own good. I know you, honey. If you witnessed any questionable behavior, you'd stick your pretty nose in their business. You couldn't help yourself. Your curiosity would demand it."

She stared at him. How would he know what happens near the Pike? Granted he lived six blocks east, but in a sophisticated development.

The lines at the corner of his eyes deepened. She walked away from him. Embarrassed over her lack of knowledge in certain areas of her life, she wanted to get out of there. Changing her plan now put a serious dent in finding a place within two weeks. She had no idea where to go to next.

"Wait, Ang," Gary called behind her.

She waved her hand over her shoulder, needing to think. Maybe she wasn't prepared to live on her own without help. The thought sat uneasy on her shoulders. Had she been naive living with Jules all these years? The thought that *her* city was unsafe depressed her.

She arrived at Gary's car first and waited by the passenger door. He slipped between her and the lock and opened the door, letting her inside. If it were anyone else witnessing her bad decision, she would've shrugged off her mistake. But this was Gary.

Anything that happened with her got back to Drew, and if she knew her brother—and she did after spending time in

Deadhorse—he'd do something dumb like move back to Seattle to try and take care of her. That's what he always did.

Gary started the car. "Are you mad?"

"No." She leaned her head back on the seat and looked at him. "Can we keep his between you and me?"

"Who would I tell?"

"Drew," she said.

He slipped his hand into hers and squeezed. "Nothing happened. I was here with you. There's nothing to tell Drew. Okay?"

She continued holding his hand and when he let her, she relaxed. Three blocks later, when his thumb caressed the back of her hand, her gaze dropped to their linked fingers. Her chest fluttered and warmth spread throughout her body. Afraid to look at him in case he was aware of what was happening to her, she held completely still.

Maybe she imagined her reaction to him comforting and supporting her.

He was a guy. Her emotions were on a roller coaster lately.

She couldn't possibly be sexually attracted to Gary. Her heart raced. She'd grown up with him. He was her buddy. Her brother's best friend. They teased each other, and she'd tried to set him up on dates with her girlfriends before.

Okay, he never agreed to date any of her friends, but she'd tried. It wasn't like she went after him herself. *Oh, God.*

She'd slept with him. Not that they had sex, but she'd woken up on top of him. Could she have done something in her sleep? Not sex, but touched him so he thought…

She shook her head and gazed out the window. No, she'd definitely remember touching him, even if she did it in her sleep. A body like his would burn on her brain. She'd remember the hardness, the warmth, the power.

The air inside the car thickened. She was definitely feeling something. To test herself, she moved her finger slightly, rearranging her hold on his hand. He loosened his grip, but continued to clasp her hand, even giving it another squeeze to reassure her that he wasn't letting go.

Pleasurable throbbing settled low in her belly and gravitated between her legs. She whipped her gaze to Gary to see if he was feeling it too. He stared out at the road, seemingly unaware of her conflicting thoughts and the way her body was out of control.

She couldn't talk to him about what was happening. He'd probably laugh at her. She needed to tell someone…someone who could view this as an outsider and tell her it was a stupid idea to even think of Gary as, as, as, someone she would like to be with.

Before she could stop her train of thought, she blurted, "Let's swing by Jules's apartment. I want to change our plans."

Gary glanced at her. "I thought we were all going out clubbing tomorrow night."

"No. Friday is a better night to go out. The crowd isn't as wild at the Metro, and Jules said the band that's been playing there lately is really good." She let go of his hand, swallowing hard for the first time since they got into the car.

Gary turned left down the next street and five minutes later, they were at her old apartment. She jumped out of the car, aware of Gary following. If anyone could help her it would be Jules. She was smart about sensing someone's feelings, and if Gary thought of her as a sister, she'd have to give up the thought of ever making a play for him.

She came up sharp at the door and stilled. *A play?*

What the hell was happening to her? She couldn't go after Gary. He was off limits.

She rapped on the door, waited a second, and knocked harder. Gary chuckled. She rolled her eyes. He had no idea she had an emergency on her hands. The more noise she made, the faster Jules would come to the door.

Impatient, she raised her hand to knock again and the door opened. Jules stared at them both, then snapped out of her surprise.

"Hey, you're back!" Jules grabbed Angie and pulled her inside, hugging her. "I've missed you. It seems like you were gone forever."

She held on to Jules, because this was her best friend. The one who supported her, gave her great advice, and wouldn't think she was completely whacked for thinking Gary was the sexiest man she'd ever seen, and she only realized it tonight when something weird happened on the sidewalk when he tried to boss her around. "Change of plans. We're going out tonight."

"But, I—"

"Have to go out with us tonight." Angie looked at Gary. "Excuse us for a moment, we'll be right back. Make yourself at home, drink some water, or watch some television…"

"Honey, you don't live here anymore." Gary's jaw twitched and he held her gaze. "Maybe Jules doesn't want us invading her place."

"It's okay. She loves me." She waved her hand. "Give us ten minutes."

Once inside Jules's bedroom and out of sight of Gary, Angie panicked. She gripped Jules's arms and shook her. "What am I going to do?"

"About what?" Jules grabbed her wrists and brought Angie's arms down. "Take a deep breath, sweetie. You're freaking, and you're starting to freak me out. What happened since you've been gone?"

"Nothing. Everything. Shit, this is wrong on so many levels." She closed her eyes for a beat, and looked at Jules straight on. "I've got a huge problem and yes, I'm freaking the freak out."

Jules led her to the bed, pushed her down, and sat beside her holding her hands. "Talk to me."

Angie stared at the floor. Once she confessed, there would be no taking it back. Her feelings would become real and with the way she was, she'd fall head over heels for Gary without thinking about the repercussions. But if she kept her secret, maybe tomorrow she'd wake up and her stomach would no longer being doing back hand springs every time Gary was around or he touched her.

Now that she thought about it, her stomach had been acting crazy since they'd driven back from Deadhorse. She'd thought it was hunger, cravings, and tried to fill the void with Doritos and red licorice, but she was insatiable. She was still hungry. For Gary.

Jules shook her hands. "Angie…tell me."

She inhaled a shuddering breath, and sagged against her friend. "I think I want Gary."

There. She'd set her life in motion. There was no stopping her feelings now.

Chapter Eight

Gary stood between Angie and Jules inside the Metro, searching over the heads of the customers for an empty table. Angie glanced at Jules, and received a conspiracy wink in return.

Angie ran her hand over her stomach and inhaled a shaky breath. It was time.

After explaining to Jules earlier in the day about all the quivers, flip-flops, and tingles in her body lately when she was around Gary, and hearing Jules's honest verdict in favor of her being unquestionably attracted to Gary, Angie had filled Jules in on her plan to test out her theory. This new fascination had to be tested and verified by an outside person. She couldn't make a mistake, or she'd hurt one of the most important people in her life.

Make that two important people. If her brother found out what was happening to her, what she planned to do to Gary, he'd kick her butt.

Tonight, Jules would find ways to observe Gary and her together, scope him for any sign that he was returning her feelings, and if everything moved according to Angie's prediction, Jules would put her stamp of approval on going forward. What Angie would do with the big push to move forward, putting the moves on Gary…well, she had no idea what she'd do.

"There's a table in the back, ladies." Gary motioned Jules ahead of him, and put his hand on Angie's back.

Sign one. He wasn't touching Jules. He was touching her. Angie's nipples peaked. Definitely sign one.

Angie leaned in closer and smiled up at Gary. He wasn't looking at her, because he was busy parting the crowd and keeping her safely tucked against his side. Unaware if any of her old friends were at the club, she was content to stay with Gary.

At the table, Gary held her chair and sat down on the same side, opposite of Jules. Angie bugged her eyes at her friend. Was this a sign?

Paranoia crept up her spine. She'd known Gary longer. That was why he'd sit beside her. It wasn't the first time. He often stood, sat, leaned against a wall when she was around. They were friends. Friends did that sort of thing.

"What do you girls want to drink?" Gary leaned back in his chair and put his arm across the back of her chair.

Her heart rate matched the music. *Boom, boom, boom, bang!*

"Cosmo," Jules said. "I can get my own though. Don't worry about me."

"I've got it tonight. It's Angie's welcome home party." Gary turned to Angie. "What do you want, honey?"

Honey. Sign number two.

It wasn't the first time he used the endearment directed at her. Now that she thought about it, he said it a lot during their conversations. Only to her, and never Jules. How long had he known Jules? Three, four years? Certainly enough time to give her an endearment, right?

She melted and leaned her shoulder into his side. "I'll have the same, and a basket of chips with salsa...since you're buying."

His body shook against her, and he lowered his mouth to her ear. "I'll order you nachos topped with meat. The added protein will be good for you, since you refused dinner back at the condominium."

Of course she'd refused to eat with him. Her insides were a jumbled mess, and it wasn't food she required.

"Your concern for the size of my ass is touching," she whispered back, grinning.

He laughed, keeping his mouth at the side of her head. "Your ass is perfect. I'm more concerned about you having something in your stomach if you're planning on drinking."

Bells rang in her head. Sign number three. He liked her ass.

"I'll make sure I share my nachos." She leaned back and smiled. "If I'm going out of this life doing what I enjoy, I'd rather do it loaded in comfort food."

His smile fell and his mouth hardened. She glanced between him and Jules. Had she said something wrong?

They were joking. She'd already told him she didn't live off junk food alone. He couldn't possibly be upset over her snack cravings, could he?

"Hey." Jules sat straighter and waved. "There's a waitress."

While Gary ordered and his attention was off her, Angie mouthed *what's going on?* to Jules. Jules shrugged, then she raised her eyebrows and held up a finger for her to wait. Angie settled back and tried to listen to the band. Her emotions were all over the place, making the task impossible.

A new job. A new place to live. A new attraction. No wonder she craved junk food. Gary had no understanding of how a woman worked. She sucked in her breath. It wouldn't surprise her if something big happened and her world exploded.

The waitress returned. Angie smiled her thanks, and lifted the glass to her mouth at the same time Jules shoved the table, which bumped her elbow, and liquid sloshed out of her drink onto the front of her shirt.

"Oh shit, I'm sorry, Ang." Jules scooped up the napkins on the table and shoved them at Gary. "I thought the tables were bolted down."

"It's okay." She pulled her shirt away from her bra, hoping to stop the wetness from going any further.

Gary patted above her shirt on her chest. She let go of her shirt, watching his broad hand in fascination. Strong, thick, long fingers made the napkin all but hidden. She gasped as he went lower, dabbing at the front of her shirt, between her breasts. Her nipples constricted pleasurably and her gaze shot up to Gary's face. He concentrated on the front of her, his gaze heated and intense.

Her chest rose and fell, matching the crazed reaction to his touch. Barely aware of the others in the room or Jules watching the whole moment, she laid her hand atop Gary's. He lifted his gaze and in that moment, she positively knew he had the same feelings as her. Without breaking his gaze, she leaned forward. He tossed the napkin, and brought his hand to the back of her neck, pulling her closer.

"Honey?" he mumbled, his lips hovering over hers.

She nodded slightly and moistened her lips, giving him permission to kiss her. Warmth from his breath settled over her, and she closed her eyes, waiting, wanting, wigging out because the only thing she wanted this second was Gary's lips on hers.

"Fuck," he whispered.

The rush of air from the curse opened her eyes. Gary scraped back his chair and left the table. She stared after him, unsure what happened. He was right there with her, feeling the same thing she was, and then he was gone.

"Oh, girlfriend. That was the best almost kiss I have ever seen in my life. Pure movie scene." Jules lifted her drink in the air. "Did you see the way he took control and pulled you toward him?"

"Yeah," she whispered, watching Gary talk to the bartender across the room and lean his elbows down on the counter. "Why did he leave?"

"I don't know, but forget about collecting the seven signs of attraction. The vehemence behind his actions shoved him right into the he's-got-it-bad-for-you category." Jules waved her hand in front of her face. "God, it's hot in here. You two were steaming it up."

"Maybe he's mad?" Angie tore her gaze away from Gary and looked to Jules. "There was nothing stopping him from kissing me. I even closed my eyes. I gave him every signal that I wanted him."

Jules blew out her cheeks and let the air go. "He's fighting himself for some reason, but you can't give up on him. You need to find out what he's thinking. Maybe it's something stupid like he's worried about starting anything with you because football season starts soon. Or he's looking for one night of slapping skin, and you live with him, so he's trying to be a gentleman."

"That's true." She nodded. "In three days, practice starts for him, and I start my new job. That's probably it. I guess it's bad timing on my part."

But what if his schedule wasn't the problem? She'd asked him if he had a girlfriend, and he told her no. Beyond that, she had no idea what or who was involved in his life.

"Do you want me to go talk with him?" Jules reached across the table and squeezed her hand.

Angie inhaled deeply through her nose. "No. I'll talk to him."

Gathering her courage, she stood from the table and wound her way across the club. She lost sight of Gary through the crowd, and excused herself through the groups gathered around the dance floor.

Shoved from behind, she bumped into a man. "I'm sorry."

The man turned around. She smiled in delight and jumped into his arms. She hadn't seen Dave Trand since she was laid off from work. He was one of her former clients.

"How are you?" She stepped back to see him better. "Look at you. Your back doing better?"

A few inches taller than her, he stood straight and confident. A grin lit up his face, and he held out his arms to the side, letting her get her fill of his body. She nodded, pleased with what she was seeing.

He twisted at the waist. "I received a clean bill of health to return to work three weeks ago, and I'm giving all the credit to you. I couldn't have made the progress without you helping me along the way."

After a severe car accident that broke the C5 vertebra, Dave came in to the spa and received a massage three times a week for over a year. She rubbed his arm, thrilled over the changes in Dave. "I'm so happy to hear that. Gosh, it's great to see you. I've wondered how you were getting on, and you've made my day. Wonderful news."

He kissed her cheeks. "I heard about the job and the spa closing. Is everything okay?"

"Yeah." She grinned. "Even better than okay. Starting Monday, I'm working with the Seattle Seahawks."

Dave rocked back on the heel of his shoes and laughed. "Well deserved. Congratulations."

"Thank you. I'm excited and—"

A hand hooked her elbow. She turned and found Gary standing beside her. "Dave, this is Gary Satchel, one of the—"

"Only the best defenseman in the NFL." Dave pumped Gary's offered hand. "Nice to meet you, man."

"Same here." Gary looked down at Angie. "Are you ready to go?"

She racked her teeth over her bottom lip. "We haven't been here very long, and I thought we'd spend some time listening to the band and dancing."

"I'll let you two have your privacy." Dave stepped back. "Great to see you again, Angie."

"You too." She smiled, but when she turned back to Gary he was watching her closely. "What?"

"You want to dance…we'll dance." Gary led her further out onto the floor.

He swept her into his arms. She wrapped her arms around his waist to keep her balance. He turned her into a spin, and she couldn't grasp what he was doing.

"You don't dance," she said, saying the first thing that popped into her head.

She'd asked him before when they'd met up at the same club on the same night. Not once had he danced with her or any other woman that she knew about.

He shrugged. "If you want to dance, I'll be the one you dance with…not Dave whoever he is that you were hugging."

She stiffened and gazed up at his face. "Dave Trand is happily married, and a previous client of mine."

He grunted. "Doesn't matter."

Dawning came swiftly. She giggled and held on to him tighter. "You're jealous."

"No." He gazed over her head. "I'm protective. Your brother placed you in my care, and I'd do anything for Drew. Including making sure you don't go off with some guy you barely know—"

"I've known Dave for over a year." She grinned, loving the way he tried to explain away his reaction. "Drew even knows him."

"Well, Drew isn't here, is he?" He dropped his chin to his chest and looked at her. "I thought you wanted to dance. We're not moving."

That was true. They stood clutched in each other's arms, their feet still, the music absent. She wiggled out of his embrace, grabbed his hand, and pulled him through the crowd. She wasn't into making his life miserable. If he preferred to sit on the sidelines, she'd sit with him.

Back at the table, Jules was gone. Angie's pocket vibrated, and she pulled out her phone.

Found Steph, we're going to the Dax. Sorry. Make it right with G. Make it up to U later. XXOO

She sighed and typed back. *Loser. Call me tmrw.*

"What's going on?" Gary sat down.

She swiveled in her chair. "Jules left with Stephanie—remember her?"

He nodded. "Blonde, crazy, and always wears that black hat."

"A beret. Yeah, that's her. Jules dumped us." She slouched. "I guess we can go home."

No more than twenty minutes later, after splitting the nachos between them, Gary ushered her to his car and they were driving back to his condominium in silence. The evening ended on a downer. She stared out the window and contemplated her next plan. Except, she had no idea which direction to go. Maybe she should forget about pursuing her feelings and concentrate on her new job instead.

Chapter Nine

What the hell am I doing?

Gary stood in front of the window in his bedroom. He gazed out at the city lights, not seeing anything but his messed up life. He'd almost kissed Angie tonight.

Always having gone after what he wanted, he struggled between letting Angie know flat out that he wanted her or walking away from their friendship entirely. He leaned his head against the glass. It was more than that. He loved her.

For years he'd wanted her, but what he was feeling went past temptation and getting his nut off. His feelings for her had never been at the friend level. There'd always been something about her that caused him to put her up there in his head where no one could touch her. Old girlfriends paled compared to Angie. She was the scale in which he measured every woman. He continually tried dating, hoping he'd lose his feelings for Angie, but he could never think about his dates for longer than one night.

In fact, the last woman he'd dated became obsessed with him. He'd tried to let her down easy, but he actually understood how she was feeling, because of his feelings for Angie. What a fucking mess. He needed to straighten his head out.

He just couldn't figure out why. What was there about her that made him latch on to a fantasy? She never treated him any differently than any of Drew's other friends. He closed his eyes. That wasn't true.

She'd needed him. Right before her mom died, they'd grown closer. She'd relied on him for strength. It was back when he was spending every minute at Drew's house, instead of at his foster house. In the middle of the night when she paced her room, worried about her mom, he'd sit in the hallway and talk with her.

Not about what was happening. It was all about silly stuff girls think about, and he had no interest in.

Except he listened and he cared, because it was what Angie was interested in.

After Mrs. Swanson's death, their closeness remained, but he was positive that Angie never thought of him in the same way he did. He was so careful to keep everything he was feeling to himself. Drew would've hated him for making a play for his little sister.

But it was more than not encroaching on a sacred friendship. He'd needed her more than she needed him. He connected on an emotional level with her, and she had no idea how she'd balanced his anger over his life, his mom, his sucky teenaged life. Without her, he would've slipped inside himself and hated the whole world. She gave him something to achieve, and kept his head on straight.

Then tonight, his whole goal of keeping his distance went away. He swore Angie put the moves on him. She leaned into him every chance she had. That tender smile—the one she rarely gave, preferring to let others see her more carefree and silly attitude—hit him square in the gut twice tonight.

He opened his eyes and turned away from the window. He dived onto the bed and groaned. Was he willing to throw away the only family he gave a damn about to see if Angie saw anything in him?

To do so would gamble with his happiness. Drew's happiness. Hell, Angie's happiness if she thought of him as only a friend.

A soft knock interrupted his musings. His whole body tensed. She'd fallen asleep two hours ago. He'd checked.

He pushed himself to his feet and strode across the room. Before he opened the door, he looked down. He'd stripped down to his boxers earlier. Another knock came, and he brushed off his lack of clothing. She'd seen him in his underwear lots of times, and she appeared to have no problems with that.

He opened the door.

She gazed up at him. He refrained from saying anything or giving her any clue on where his thoughts were tonight. One sign, one gesture, one touch, and he'd have her on her back underneath him and his cock sunk deep inside her body.

Without a word, she walked past him and climbed up on the bed. Her ass wiggled as she crawled atop the mattress to the far side closest to the window and snuggled under the covers. He raised his gaze to the ceiling, pleading for death. He'd never make it until morning without touching her.

He quietly closed the door, and walked over to the bed. Like last night, he laid on top of the covers on his back. He clasped his hands behind his head, and went over football plays in his head.

Unlike last night, Angie remained quiet. No questions or speculations came from the other side of the bed. No wacky questions he had no answers to or that made him laugh no matter how hard he tried not to. The change set heavy on his chest.

More than an hour went by, listening to Angie's breathing soften and slow. He closed his eyes, knowing he had to get some sleep. The first week of practice always kicked his ass and without enough rest, he'd suffer.

Forcing his breathing to relax, he heeded Angie's example and let himself sleep.

Sometime later, he woke and held still. Aware of Angie in his room, he moved his hand to his stomach, but her head wasn't laying on him. He opened his eyes and searched the bed, knowing something had woken him up.

Across the expanse of mattress, Angie whimpered in her sleep. He rolled to his side to watch her. She was probably dreaming and would settle down soon. Waking her up would only interrupt her sleep more.

She squirmed, fighting the blankets, until she thrust them off her upper body and got on her hands and knees. He sat up, alarmed, but something held him back.

Angie used both her hands to push on the mattress as if squishing the springs down. He moved closer and laid his hand on her back. "Ang?" he whispered. "What are you doing, honey?"

She jolted, falling back on her butt, crying out in pain. He held up his hands. "It's me. Gary."

A low moan erupted and she pitched herself at him. He caught her, and she buried her face in his neck. He was fully awake now.

What the hell happened to her?

"Shh." He scooted back until he leaned against the headboard and pulled her onto his lap, not letting her go. "Everything's okay. I got you."

Her whole body trembled. He ran his hand down her back. The other one cupped the back of her head. Worried something had happened while he was asleep, he kept talking nonsense.

"Are you in pain?" he asked.

She rubbed her face back and forth against his chest. He sensed moisture on his skin and realized she was crying. Useless and unprepared, he had no idea how to make her feel better.

He kissed the top of her head. "Did you have a bad dream?"

She stiffened, holding on to him tightly. He took that as a yes. His rising panic eased back down to concern. A nightmare he could handle.

"I'll get you a drink of water…" He shifted to set her on the bed, and she raised her head, anxiety etched around her eyes. "It's okay, I'll be right back."

She nodded shakily.

"Okay." He kissed her forehead. "I'll turn on the hall light and leave the bedroom door open while I go to the kitchen."

He hurried out of the room, hit the light switch on his way down the hall, and continued on his way to get some water. On his way back to the bedroom, he hoped to find her asleep but when he cleared the door, she was sitting on the edge of the bed wiping her face.

"Here you go." He handed her the glass and sat beside her.

Her hand shook, and he put his arm behind her and rubbed her back. Slowly, she stopped trembling and emptied the glass. He carried the cup to the dresser and returned to the bed.

Without telling her to get back on her side of the bed, he lay down and took her with him. He pulled her back against his chest, and wrapped his arm around her waist. She took his hand with both of hers, and clutched it between her breasts. His legs molded with hers. Holding her this way reminded him how tiny she was compared to him.

A better man would've put any sexual thoughts out of his mind. She was scared and upset after having a bad dream, and needed comfort. A friend would give her the security of knowing she could rest and he'd protect her from whatever dream bothered her sleep.

Not him.

The hollow spot between her breasts swallowed his hand, surrounding him in warmth, the kind of heat that only came from having a woman's body holding his. Her ass fit perfectly in the curve of his body. Her smooth legs were like silk against his hairier ones. He wasn't immune to the differences.

She smelled of warm vanilla, reminding him of the scent he picked up at the club when he was close enough to kiss her and had him dreaming of the possibilities of having his feelings reciprocated.

He hardened at the thought.

He also breathed heavy against her ear.

He was out of control.

He was an asshole.

She didn't need to worry about him right now or what was pressing against her backside, or him wishing she'd roll over so he could—

Tied. I'm facing off with Kanu from the Steelers. There's blood in his eyes. I bend low and dive for his legs. Kanu fumbles the ball…

Shit. Football will not help me. I'm calling Drew in the morning.

Chapter Ten

Gary checked his phone for the fourth time since leaving the condo. Angie walked beside him toward the practice field in Renton, north of Seattle. He'd closed himself off all morning, and since she'd spent Saturday with Jules alone, and shopping for more appropriate clothes for her new job on Sunday, she had no idea what was bothering him.

Ever since she made a fool of herself after having a nightmare about losing her mother again while sleeping in his bed on Friday night, she'd fought the funk that permeated her days. As soon as practice was over and she was alone, she'd call Drew. Maybe after talking with him, finding out if she was crazy or not, she'd know how to approach Gary about her attraction to him.

Attraction. Such a silly word for what was happening to her. She wanted him, and for more than just sex. She loved having him in her life, and missed him when they were apart. Jules might be her best friend when it came to everyday life and girl fun, but Gary was a constant. He was the one person she allowed herself to feel vulnerable around, and she never realized how much until she spent twenty-four hours a day with him.

With him, she wasn't uptight, driven, focused on all the menial things that distracted her from living life. He gave her hope and confidence to stick with a plan and see it through. She was here, working for the Seahawks, because of him. She'd survived her teenage years because of him. In the back of her mind, she had a deep sense of security around him, and it had been placed there years ago, by him.

And it scared her to death.

Her fear of losing another person in her life—and she knew it was irrational—kept her from so many things. That was something she didn't allow anyone to know. Not Drew, not Jules, and not Gary.

Except, Gary would find out if she continued sleeping with him and she kept waking up having the same damn nightmare she'd had since she was eighteen years old. She sighed and stopped at the sidelines to the field.

"Nervous?" Gary shoved his phone into his bag and tossed it to the ground.

She inhaled deeply and shrugged. "A little. I'm supposed to meet John in a half hour. Apparently Hagman is returning with a strained hamstring. I'll be working on him today. My first foray into working with guys twice the normal size of the males I usually worked on."

"Hagman's small." Gary studied her, seeming to want to say something more.

"What?"

He shook his head. "Nothing."

"No, it's something. What were you going to say?" She laid her hand on his arm. "You've been quiet the last couple of days. Is it something you want to talk about, or I should ignore you because it's normal pre-season stress?"

He gazed out on the field where his teammates tossed a football around, warming up and waiting for the start of practice. "Watch out for the guys. They can act like assholes around a woman."

She laughed softly. "I think I understand how boys act. I grew up with you and Drew, right?"

"Yeah," he muttered. "Just let me know if anyone steps out of bounds."

She nudged his arm with her shoulder. "You sound like my brother going all overprotective."

"I'm not your brother." He walked off, looping into a jog as he hit the fifty-yard line to join the others.

She couldn't win lately. Nothing she said or did helped get Gary in a better mood. She glanced at her phone to check the time, and decided calling Drew with the remaining twenty minutes she had until John showed up would save her time later.

She hit the button and held the phone to her ear. On the third ring, Drew picked up.

"Hey, sis."

"Hey." She smiled, genuine warmth filling her. She missed his ugly mug. "Can I just say that getting out of Deadhorse was the best thing for me?"

He laughed. "Happy, huh?"

"Yeah…" She watched Gary throw a football in a perfect arched spiral through the air. "What have you been doing?"

"Same ol'. Decided to paint the garage, since I took in two custom jobs in the past week," he said.

"That's great." She shoved her free hand in the front pocket of her yoga shirt. "Did the gas company change their rotation to Thursdays for you?"

"Yeah, I had no problems changing the contract." He paused. "You didn't call me to talk about the garage. What's up?"

She turned away from the field, and even though Gary wasn't paying attention to her now, she felt guilty for talking behind his back. "What do you know about Gary's love life?"

Drew cussed. "How am I supposed to know?"

"I'm serious, Drew." She paused, waiting, but he didn't seem in a hurry to spill his secrets. "Come on, I'm curious. I know he talks to you."

"Does this have anything to do with him calling me about fifty times since Saturday morning? He keeps catching me asleep or with my hands covered in grease. What did he do, get himself stuck with some chick who became obsessed with him like the last woman he dated?"

"What?" She shook her head. "No. What girl?"

"Old news. He had a woman he dated a few times about a year ago, and she wanted something more and started stalking him. That's why he moved to the gated condominiums. He was tired of answering his door at all hours of the day and night to find her wanting to visit," Drew said.

"Oh geez, that's awful." She paced as she continued. "No, I don't think he has a problem with a girlfriend. He says he's not seeing anyone."

"He never 'sees' someone. That's not Gary's way. I think it has to do with the way he grew up, and living with the losers who called themselves his foster parents. He's not big on relationships or getting serious. Not that he doesn't have his share of women; he has more than he needs."

"About that…" She sat down on a nearby bench. "Don't you think he'd be happy if he was in a relationship?"

"Are you serious?" Drew said.

"I mean, he's a great guy. We both know that. He deserves to have someone in his life to make him happy," she said.

"I won't argue with that, but I'm going to stop you right now, because I know you. You're going to drive him insane, and it's the wrong time for you to be a pain in his ass. So tell your friend you're not going to set Gary up with her. He doesn't do blind dates."

"But what if it's someone special?" She wrinkled her nose, knowing how stupid she was being by not coming right out and saying it was about her, not a friend. "Let's just speculate for a second. Say the girl is just like me, and she's in it because she's serious. No fooling around, no playing games, and not out to screw him over. Do you think Gary is open to getting to know someone…like me?"

"Fuck, I don't know, sis." Drew heaved a breath over the phone. "Guys don't discuss what they want in a woman besides looks, brains, and how to spot one who knows not to talk too much."

"Funny, jerk." She dropped her chin to her chest and lowered her voice. "Believe it or not, I only want what is best for Gary."

"Angie. Think about what you're doing. You've had a lot going on in your life. You're starting a new job, finding a new place to live, and the stress from the last few months are finally catching up to you. Don't ruin your friendship with Gary over some fleeting idea you've got in your head that you can make his life better," Drew said. "Concentrate on your life."

"I think I know what I'm doing," she whispered.

Several seconds went by with neither one of them saying anything. Finally Drew spoke. "Then talk to him first. Make sure you do it in terms he understands, not your usual back and forth way of talking. No guy wants to have a woman thrown at him and be taken by surprise."

"Yeah?" She raised her gaze to the field.

Drew chuckled. "Yeah. Remember the last time you set one of your friends up with me?"

She groaned. "I am sorry about that. Samantha was not who I thought she was."

"I still love you." Drew muffled the phone and came back on the line. "Listen, I got a customer. I need to go."

"Okay." She stood and walked back toward the players' bench. "Thanks, Drew. I'll talk to you in a few days."

"Hey, before you hang up, Dad called."

"About?"

"He was looking for you. I told him you'd moved back to Seattle. He wants to talk to you about keeping the kids again," Drew said.

She closed her eyes; she'd barely survived the last time she babysat them. "Okay, I'll watch for his call."

"Cool," Drew said. "Talk to you later."

"Bye."

She shoved the phone back in her pocket. Teak Swanson, her father, always went about life at his own pace. Unable to settle down while he was married to her mom, they quickly divorced, while he traveled the world. His second wife seemed to keep him by her side, but she enjoyed traveling as much as he did, which meant the kids were foisted off on either Angie or Drew while they were gone. She loved her half siblings, but it took constant supervision and she had no idea how she'd manage to watch them with a new job.

"Angie Swanson?" A male voice came from behind her.

She turned and smiled. "Yes, I'm Angie."

"John." He shook her hand. "Great to have you on board. Should we get started?"

"Absolutely," she replied.

Dressed in jeans and a Seahawk sweatshirt, John led the way to the other end of the field. Tall, fit, and longish blond hair curling around his neck fooled her for a minute. He looked nothing like any physical therapist she'd met. But his easygoing attitude put her at ease as just another guy who enjoyed football.

Chapter Eleven

Gary's stomach heaved. He bent at the waist, bracing himself on his knees. Finishing the 40-60-80 sprints signaled the end of practice for the day. Three hours of hell, where he pushed his body to the extreme, and he loved every minute of it.

He hurt in more places than he was aware of before practice. The contents of his stomach, which was mostly water, threatened to come up. Most people believed he put his sweat and blood in the games, and they were right. They called it conditioning for a reason, and it wasn't unusual to dislocate a finger, slice open a knee, or puke your guts out on the sidelines.

If Coach asked him to get down to a six point—hands, knees, feet, and crouch—he'd probably topple over, he was that tired. But, he'd survived the day and he'd be ready for more on Wednesday.

"Shit, man. I need answers." McCormick sucked wind down the line from Gary. "Someone has got to get me that girl's phone number."

Beside him, Yeager answered. "What girl?"

"The new lady with the magic fingers," McCormick said, grabbing his crotch. "I think I pulled a muscle."

"Bullshit," Gary shot back. "Wimping out is more like it. Suck it up, cupcake, season's only beginning."

He'd heard the talk the last hour. Every single man and half the men already taken eyed Angie any time they got a free second. He couldn't blame them, but he hated it. Deciding to keep his roommate status secret, so to keep everyone away from Angie, he checked himself anytime she was mentioned. If they knew she was a friend of his, and stayed at his place, they'd be stopping by all the time.

He started the long walk back to the other side of the field to grab his bag. All he could think about was going home, sinking down into the hot tub, and crashing for a few hours until he forgot about the exhaustion.

Hell, he couldn't even imagine next week when they actually put their pads on and scrimmaged with the extra weight on his body. He'd survive and be better for it, but every year got tougher, the players younger, bigger, and he was only getting older.

As he reached his bag, took out a towel, and mopped his head off, he kept his eye on Angie. Twenty yards away, she stood talking with John and Benton, the quarterback. Both men laughed at something Angie said, and she smiled, shaking her head in pure happiness. Jealousy sparked inside him. Of course everyone liked her. She was perfect.

But she belonged to him. At least until she found her own place to live.

"Hey, Angie," he called.

She turned, waved, spoke with John and Benton, then jogged over to him. He hung his towel around his neck. The other guys watched him, and he turned his back to them.

"You ready to go?" he said. "I'm skipping the locker room and heading straight home before I pass out."

"Yeah. I'm ready." She picked up his bag with a groan.

His hand closed around hers on the handle. "What are you doing?"

"You're exhausted. I'll carry the bag, and you can concentrate on walking to the car," she said.

He took the duffle from her. "I can handle it."

They walked together. Angie glanced at him, fairly bouncing with each step. His body screamed in protest, but he could damn well carry his own bag. He wasn't helpless.

At the car, he tossed his stuff in the back seat, and leaned against the car for a moment to gather his strength. His legs had turned into jelly fifty paces back and his head swam. He needed to hydrate.

She studied him over the roof of the car. "You okay?"

"Beat." He grinned. "It's like this every year. If I survive the first week, there's a good chance I'll live."

"Poor baby." She bit down on her bottom lip. "The big, bad pro football player is tired…"

"I'd walk over there and spank you for that if I could make my feet move." He shook his head. "Right now, I'll be thankful if I make it to the hot tub."

"Do you want me to drive?" she asked.

For a second, he honestly contemplated letting her slide behind the wheel of his Camaro. "No, once I sit down, I'll be fine."

A half hour later when he climbed out of the car, he regretted his stubbornness. Every muscle screamed in protest. He would've felt better if he walked the entire distance home and not let his muscles tighten up.

In the kitchen, he peeled off his shirt. In the living room, he toed off his cleats and over exerted himself. Angie or not, he was going to be bare ass naked by the time he hit his bedroom and slipped out the sliding door onto the balcony where the hot tub sat.

"Go ahead and soak." Angie unzipped his bag. "I'll throw your things in the washing machine and make you a couple of sandwiches to eat. Then you can sleep."

He nodded, or maybe he didn't. He couldn't be sure, because even that much movement hurt as he dragged his feet across the floor.

Thankfully, he'd known the condition he'd be in when he returned home and earlier had removed the top off the hot tub. All he had to do was climb two steps and ease himself into the water. He stood on the deck, eyeing the steps as if he were a geriatric patient who'd only snapped out of a drug-induced coma an hour ago and had yet to figure out how to move his feet.

Eventually, he made it to the top, heaved his leg over the side, and slid down into the jetted water. His body seized and quickly succumbed to the power of the warmth in blessed relief. He sighed long and loud. At that moment, nothing compared to how he was feeling. Not even sex or winning the Super Bowl felt better.

He let his head fall back on his shoulders and he closed his eyes. His arms half floated out to the sides. All his muscles gave away their tight control and he succumbed to the weightlessness of the water. Only then was he able to breathe without any pain.

Today's practice pushed him, and despite the soreness, being back in the routine that he loved felt good. Angie's presence in his life upset the balance, in a good way, but even thinking hurt when he'd given one hundred and ten percent on the field. But with the season also came the control he needed to keep his head in the game, and hopefully distance himself from Angie.

He thought about Drew and all the phone calls that went unanswered. It wasn't uncommon for it to take days to make a connection. They both lived busy lives, and they were guys. They rarely called to chitchat. If he left a message and told Drew it was important to return his call, he had no doubt Drew would contact him. He just wasn't ready to come clean.

Once he took a snooze, he'd try calling the gas station again. He'd feel out Drew for any sign that he would raise hell if Gary put the moves on Angie. He dunked his head, and came up shaking the water out of his hair. It was going to be a long season if the other players kept on with their fascination over Angie.

"Sit up." Angie materialized beside him. He hadn't even heard her come out over the noise from the jets in the tub.

She handed him a towel. "Wipe your hands off, and you can eat while you relax."

"Not very hungry yet." He took one of the sandwiches off the plate. "But thanks. I know I'll be starving in an hour."

She climbed up on the step, and perched on the side of the hot tub. Despite the exhaustion and the high temperature of the water, his body hardened instantly.

"Uh, honey, I don't have shorts on." He popped the last bite into his mouth.

She handed him the second sandwich. "I know."

To his surprise, she glanced down at the water. Holy shit. She was looking. It took all of his willpower not to stretch out fully or stand up and let her see. He was proud of his body. More importantly, he had the mother lode of all hard-ons, and he wanted to show it off.

"Anybody ever tell you curiosity killed the cat?" he said, trying his best to ignore her.

She laughed softly. "Sure, but I also was told recently that to cross the end zone, you have to put your head down and run, giving it everything you've got."

"Huh?" He wiped his mouth off with his hand. "What does that mean?"

She rolled her eyes and hopped off the edge of the tub. He watched her close the sliding door and go inside the condo. End zone? Giving it everything?

Fuck. She was talking his language, and he sat here like an idiot.

He pulled himself out of the water, wrapping the towel around his hips, and grabbed his phone from where he'd left it on the lawn chair. Drew better answer the damn phone. He had an emergency on his hands.

If he was going to move forward with Angie and be honest, he needed to talk to Drew first.

The ringing stopped. Drew answered, "Yo."

"Where the hell have you been?" Gary clutched the ends of the towel.

"Working," Drew said. "Some of us don't play for gold and diamonds for a living."

Gary grunted. Now that he had Angie's brother on the phone, he had no idea how to broach the subject.

"Everything okay with Ang?" Drew asked.

"Yeah." Gary cleared his throat. "She started work today and seems to like it. The players have definitely noticed her."

Drew cussed. "Assholes."

"Exactly." Gary leaned against the railing, peering out into the woodsy area behind the gated community.

"So, what's so important, you filled my voicemail over the weekend?"

Gary blurted, "I've got a problem."

"What can I do?"

He stooped over and leaned against his elbows. This was why Drew was his best friend. He never questioned, yelled, argued, or bullied. His quiet acceptance and position in his life was to support and back him. He never took that friendship for granted.

"It's not easy living with your sister," he said.

Drew laughed. "Tell me about it."

"I'm serious, Drew. I think she's messed up. Something big is going on in her head and making her act crazy." He rubbed his hand over his face.

"Talk to me," Drew said, quietly.

He sighed without saying anything. What he and Angie talked about was between the two of them, no one else. There were certain things she probably wouldn't appreciate him saying, especially to her brother. He had to come clean with Drew about his feelings, and leave Angie out of the conversation.

"Your sister's an attractive woman." He squeezed his eyes shut. God, he sounded like a prick. Attractive didn't begin to describe her. Hot, sexy, luscious, fantasy material...

"Good looks run in the family, man." Drew laughed.

"I'm serious," he said. "The guys on the team are noticing. You know your sister; she's going to fall for their bullshit and we'll have more trouble on our hands. With the season going now and her always with the team, massaging them, there will be times I'm not around to protect her."

Silence.

His chest tightened and he exhaled his held breath. "I'm thinking it wouldn't be a bad idea to start a rumor that I'm dating Angie. Hell, she already lives with me, it wouldn't be hard to drop a few hints and let them see her with me."

Jesus. He couldn't do it. All he had to do is blurt out the truth that he loved Angie, and he chickened out.

"I just want you to know that it's not the easiest thing having her in my house, in my life twenty-four/seven, in my business," he said, mouthing *in my bed.*

Drew's breath came heavy over the phone. "Do what you have to do. I trust you."

"I know you do, but—"

"Listen. Angie's an adult. You know if I stepped into her life and told her how to live it she'd kick my ass and make sure I suffered for a week," Drew said. "Maybe you should keep your plan from her. It might go over smoother."

"Right…"

"Just don't play her. You're family and the bottom line is, I don't want something to happen where one of you gets hurt, and it breaks up my family. You get me?" Drew waited for his answer.

"I hear you." He pushed off the railing.

"Okay."

Gary stretched his back. "Thanks for talking to me."

"No problem. Talk to you later."

"Bye." He hung up.

Gary stared at the sliding door. Instead of coming clean, he'd stepped right into the fire. Though if he did pretend Angie belonged to him it'd keep the other guys away. But…

He cussed under his breath.

He couldn't spread rumors and his hands were tied in the situation. The players had a contract that they wouldn't become involved with any of the employees of the Seattle Seahawks. *Shit.*

Why hadn't he realized that sooner? He knew the rules. Angie was off limits. If they even suspected they were dating, Angie would lose her job.

Chapter Twelve

Angie paced the length of Gary's bedroom, nibbling on the corner of her fingernail. Determination fueled her. She was going to have to pump up her attempt. Gary needed to know she was open and willing to start a relationship with him.

No one night stand. No fling for the rest of their time together. No weekend dating. She wanted him permanently in her life. Yes, her decision to go for it with him had come out of the blue. She could no more explain her reasons of upsetting her life by loving a professional athlete and friend than she could her irrational fear of feeling like if she didn't do something right this minute, she'd lose him.

The sliding door slid open. Gary stopped inside the bedroom at the sight of her.

She pointed to the huge monstrosity taking up most of the room. "Lay on your bed."

He raised his brows and stayed in the same spot, not moving an inch. The heat from his gaze scorched her. With her own desire staring back at her, she knew exactly what she had to do. She held out her hand. When he took a step forward and latched on to her, she led him to the bed.

A low hum came from Gary, resembling a growl. She pushed him forward and he fell flat on his stomach, the towel around his hips landing on the floor. Before she chickened out, she climbed on top of him and sat on his bare ass.

"Ang?" he mumbled into the mattress. "Doing?"

"Giving you a hundred and fifty dollar massage." She placed her hands on his back.

Behind him, she smiled, proud that she'd wrangled him into bed, naked and hot. She ignored the fact she was too afraid to blurt out the truth. She was talented with her hands, and she'd let her fingers do her talking for her. By the time she finished, if Gary hadn't rolled over and confessed his true feelings, she would know all was lost between them.

She spread her fingers wide and swept the flat of her palm along the length of his back. She swallowed hard. His warm skin, hard muscles, and broad width gave her a large area to work on. She slowly loosened his muscles, taking her time on his lower back, running her hands over the slight indention, taking in his narrow hips, his waist, and how his upper back flared wider with the heavy muscles.

Gary moaned. She leaned forward, rounding his shoulders with the palm of her hands. Pressure from the heel of her palm followed the large cord leading up to his neck. The tension eased under her touch. Soon she moved through the motions automatically, while she let her gaze wander along his body.

She'd recognize Gary in a crowd. Probably even in a dark room. But she'd never seen him naked. Not even when she'd followed him and Drew around, tagging their every step, when she was in high school and they went to the lake and went skinny-dipping. To her disappointment, they'd found her in the back of Drew's old pickup and forced her to sit in the cab of the truck until they were finished.

A tan line ended above his buttocks. She trailed her finger over the line. Unable to take a deep breath, she said, "You're tense."

He nodded against the blanket without saying a word. Hand over hand, she pressed on a half turn of her wrist, bringing circulation to the surface, feeding his muscles the extra blood flow and oxygen they needed to unconstrict. A quiver rolled through her and she leaned forward until her breasts brushed his back. Her hands rubbed over his biceps, his forearms, his wrists, until their upper bodies lined up perfectly. Then she worked her way back until she was once again in a sitting position, her hands on his lower back.

She knew it was wrong and unprofessional to take as much pleasure as she was giving, but she couldn't stop now. "Gary? We need to talk…"

He inhaled deeply before propping himself up on his elbows. "I can't get up."

"You're still sore?" she asked, moving off him to sit beside him on the mattress.

He turned his gaze on her and the naked lust shone brighter than his bare ass. "I'm in no condition to stand up right now."

"Oh." She gulped. "Okay. That's good. I mean, fine. You lay there and I'll do the talking."

He blinked twice and nodded. "Okay."

"I'm just going to blurt everything out." She shrugged, looking over his head. "I want you to know I never planned any of this. Well, the backrub I sorta did, but not the—" she pointed back and forth between them "—you and me thing. It's not that I haven't always felt this way. I have. Kinda. Not to this degree or anything. I think it's because we've both done our own thing, and because you're Drew's friend, I took it for granted that you'd always be around. You're family."

"I'm family?" he asked.

She nodded. "Yes. No. Of course, you are. You'll always be a part of my life, and you're my friend."

"A friend?"

"Stop doing that." She sighed and eyed him. "Are you following any of this?"

"I think so." He motioned with his chin. "Hand me that towel on the floor, so I can sit up. Listening while you ogle my ass is distracting me."

She tossed him the towel and returned to the bed. "The last thing I want to do is make things uncomfortable. I should be able to ogle you without you freaking out."

"I'm not freaking out." He shook out the towel and rolled, covering himself.

"I think you are. Or maybe I am. In fact it's really burning up in here." She fanned her face with her hand. "I'm probably going to die from internal combustion. Have you ever seen that documentary? It's a real thing. One minute the person is lying there, and the next thing you know a relative found them fried to a crisp in bed. Über crazy."

Gary gawked at her. "Are you serious?"

"Totally." She shifted and sat back down crossed legged on the mattress. "Of course, I doubt if you or I will die like that, so you shouldn't worry."

"Honey." He frowned, cupping her face with his hand. "You worry me."

She closed her eyes and leaned against his touch. "I'm nervous," she whispered.

His lips touched her forehead. "I know."

"What?" She opened her eyes. "You understood what I'm trying to say?"

"Yeah." He sat down beside her, leaned forward, and braced his elbows on his knees.

Every cell in her body leapt to attention, fizzling and sending pulses erratically within her. She leaned her head against his shoulder. This was something different than they'd ever had. They'd both breached the boundary of their friendship.

Only a towel kept her from seeing all of him, and because she still wore her yoga pants, it would take her exactly five seconds to join him naked on the bed.

"It's my turn to talk." Gary stared at the floor by his feet. "Once you hear my side of things, maybe you can tell me exactly what you're thinking. No jumping from one subject to the other, no horror stories to make me worry about your sanity, and only the truth. Okay?"

She nodded.

"Good." He inhaled deeply. "A lot of this is backstory you already know. My mom gave me up to foster care and I moved around a lot until I reached junior high. That's when I met Drew. You were—"

"Twelve years old," she interrupted.

"Right." He chuckled. "I started hanging out with Drew and spending more time at your mom's house, because—"

"Your foster parents were jerks." She leaned against him. "I'm glad you became friends with Drew."

He straightened and looked at her. "Me too, but stop interrupting me because this isn't about where I came from or where I'm at now. It's the in between stage I need to tell you about. The part you don't know and can't answer me on."

"Oh…okay." She sagged against him. "Continue."

"Your mom taught me that all families are different. Whether it's a foster family, a single parent, or two parents. You make the best of what you have, and as long as there's love, everything will be fine," he said.

She crossed her arms. It'd been a long time since someone reminded her of her mother's words, and she wasn't sure how she felt about that. Part of her wanted to hear more, and her sensible side wanted to push the memories away.

"This is the important part, so listen." He lifted her chin. "You gave me something different than what I got from Drew and your mom. In you, I found understanding. Whether that was sitting in the same room as you, keeping you company while you tried so hard to take care of your mom and make sure Drew was happy, or letting you talk my ear off when the stress bottled inside of you and the only way to let it go was to talk."

"You were there for me every day," she whispered. "During that time, you'd sleep on the couch and no matter what time of the night I got up, you'd be there."

Her pulse roared in her ears. She'd hidden her feelings from everyone. How had he figured out that she'd gone to him when she couldn't handle the truth of having a mom dying of cancer and a father who was absent from her life when she needed him most?

"It was for that single reason that you gave me a purpose to keep positive about my own life. You needed me, and in the same way, I needed you." Gary cleared his throat. "Then I went away to college, you went your direction, and I lost the person that grounded me. I'll be honest. I went wild. I enjoyed the girls, the attention of being the football star, and the freedom of knowing that everyone I cared about had no idea how I was screwing up my life."

She opened her mouth, and he put his finger on her lips. "I came back to Seattle during breaks to reconnect with Drew, but it was never the same between you and me. You had outgrown your need for me. Then I graduated from college, played one season for the Steelers, got signed with the Seahawks, and spent the next three months at your house before I was scheduled to start season practice."

"And I was centered all around forgetting the blackness I'd lived through," she whispered.

He nodded. "Now keep your mouth closed until I finish, because this is probably the hardest thing I've ever had to say, and I'm afraid of fucking it up."

Okay, she mouthed.

"During that time, I fell in love with you."

Her mouth came open again, and she sucked in her lips and clamped down. Her heart raced. He loved her?

"You were out of touch for me, because you were Drew's little sister and I loved and hated how I felt about you. I betrayed everyone because of my feelings, but mostly disrespected what your family gave to me. Love and acceptance," he said.

She grabbed his hand. "But I'm not out of touch. I'm right here. That's what I've been trying to tell you. You can feel it too, can't you?"

He stood and pulled away from her, holding the towel over him. "I can't do this to us. I've never been the right man for you. You deserve someone who can give you everything—"

"What? What can't you give me?" She stood and planted her hands on her hips.

"Everything." He kept his back to her, dropped the towel, and pulled a pair of sweatpants out of the dresser, shoving his legs in the pants.

"Name something," she said.

He turned around. Anger, pain, confusion, and every other kind of emotion flickered over his face. "I'm not boyfriend or husband material. I'd make a rotten parent. I have no idea how families work, except what I learned from your family. But I was an outsider looking in, Ang. I'm a pro football player. My life is tied into the games, the money, and what comes next season."

"That's excuses." She shook her head. "I want you. Don't you understand? I don't know why it happened now, but I can't even think without wondering where you are, what you're doing, who you're thinking about."

He leaned over, picked up his T-shirt, and wadded it in his hands. "Have you read your contract?"

"What?"

"Your contract you signed when you took the job." He tossed the offending shirt across the room and watched it hit the wall. "I know in mine, I'm forbidden to date anyone employed by the owner of the Seattle Seahawks. That's you. If I dated you or they found out we were together while you were living here, you'd lose your job. They wouldn't kick me off the team, but I would end up with a fine. You though…they'd replace you."

She thrust her hands in her hair and sat back on the bed. "Shit."

"Yeah, shit." He stepped over and sat beside her. "I promise nothing will happen between us. I won't let anything ruin your chance at the job."

"But—"

"It's better this way, honey." He laid his hand over hers and squeezed. "We got a good thing going on. We're friends. Drew's my best friend. What you're feeling will go away once you get your own place. I promise."

She looked away from him. For the first time since she met him, she didn't believe a word he said.

Chapter Thirteen

The only thing yesterday's emotional talk with Gary accomplished was to make Angie more determined to figure a way out of their predicament. She followed the team toward the locker room. They'd changed fields today, putting them at the coliseum to hand out new scrimmage and game uniforms instead of at the practice field.

John cut through the throng of players toward her. "Torville needs to be rubbed down. He's on the table in the locker room."

"Great. I'll get right to it." She peered ahead at the opened double doors.

The second John turned around, she swallowed the saliva pooling in her mouth. Locker room? Her?

All kinds of scenarios played in her head. She looked around for Gary, wanting to share the monumental moment of her first time walking into a room of men who would soon be naked and showering and strutting and—she gulped—naked.

Then she realized Gary would also be stripped bare and heat consumed her face and quickly spread to her whole body. It wasn't Gary she needed to tell. Jules would be the one who'd celebrate her newfound privileges with her.

Head down, she walked through the doors with professional determination and straight toward the back of the room. A quick glance around told her that although she was out of the way from traffic, she had a clear view of the walk in showers with the half wall.

Lockers lined the perimeter of the room, followed by a row of benches. Off to the left were dressing room and closed bathrooms. She found Gary, stripping out of his shirt talking with one of the other players—number 74. He looked in her direction and raised his brows before glaring at her.

Uh oh. Obviously he'd never realized that having her working for the team would put her this close to him at all times. She swiveled around and put her hand on Tim Torville's back.

"Are you comfortable?" she asked.

Tim grunted, and remained flat on his stomach. She squatted and removed a bottle of oil from her bag under the table.

She stood and leaned over Tim. "This will feel cool on your skin after going through practice, but we don't want to cause any swelling in your muscles using heat products. It'll only take a moment and the pressure from my hands will warm you. Try to stay relaxed. It'll be enjoyable for you, and won't hurt your shoulder. If you feel yourself tensing, let me know and I can try something different."

She squirted the oil in the palm of her hand, rubbing it into her skin to warm it as much as possible. She placed her hands on Tim, and he swiftly inhaled. Within seconds, Tim relaxed again and she set about doing her job.

Being the quarterback, Tim's back wasn't as broad or as muscular as Gary's. The towel covering his hips lay low enough that she could tell he also had no tan line. She leaned over and put her elbow into his upper quadrant, manipulating the muscles. In fact, he was rather pale and freckled.

Tim moaned loud. She smiled, continuing to press into his back. There was a fine line between pleasure and pain. Experience taught her the difference between a moan and a groan. He was definitely enjoying his massage.

After causing friction to his cross muscles, she used long, flowing swipes with the heel of her hand, putting the cords of his back into proper alignment. One, two, three, she moved in precise practiced control.

Tim's moans grew louder. She shifted to her side, and leaned against the table, placing both hands on his lower back. In quick, short movements, putting weight on his back, she shook him. The guttural wail echoed in the locker room.

Accustomed to the sounds clients made during their sessions, she tuned everything out. She braced herself as she vibrated up Tim's back with her hands. His whole upper body shook, causing a warble in his voice. Near his shoulders, she stepped to the edge of the table, putting all her weight on her arms, pressing onto Tim.

The skin around Tim's neck reddened, and she slowly eased out of the movement and started petrissage, a kneading action that penetrated the deep muscles and temporarily caused a client to lose control of the area. If she asked Tim to sit up, she doubted he'd be strong enough to push himself off the table—she was that good in her work.

She removed her hands and leaned close to Tim's head. "I'm all done. Just lie there for at least ten minutes. Don't tighten your muscles. Once you're ready to get up, go slow. Sometimes a session can wipe you out."

Tim struggled to open his eyes. Without moving, he mumbled, "Thank you."

She smiled. "You're very welcome."

After putting her supplies away and zipping her bag, the silence in the locker room became apparent. Warmth crawled up her spine. She'd forgotten about her audience.

She turned.

Every player on the team stood around the room, staring at her, their hands clutching their towel or in midpoint of undressing. Three guys in the shower stood under the spray of water, watching her intently. She moistened her lips and headed straight to the bathroom area to wash her hands. Then she'd slip outside and leave them to…do whatever men did in a locker room.

At the washbowl, she soaped up her hands and rinsed off the suds. She peered up at the mirror and groaned. Her hair, windblown and messy, looked like she'd rolled out of bed and came straight to practice. She hadn't. In fact she'd spent an hour in the bathroom this morning hiding from Gary, contemplating how she'd woken up in his bed again because she hadn't remembered wandering across the hall in the middle of the night or crawling under the covers.

Yet she'd woken up on top of him. His fingers threaded through her hair, holding her in place, and she was more turned on than she'd ever been. In the car on the way over, she'd jumped every time he went to shift the car. All she could hear was her own breathing as the blood rushed through her veins.

She couldn't keep doing this to herself, or him. Something had to give, and the only thing she could come up with was to move out. She'd borrow money from him, and find herself an apartment when they got home. Even the Los Gatos club would be easier to face than another night spent with Gary and tormenting both of them.

Trying to find a loophole that'd allow her to be with Gary was proving impossible. He was a professional football player, and she had a posh job working for the team. They both had a lot to lose.

After drying her hands, she walked outside. The door hadn't even closed and Gary was on her. She backed up, and he planted his hands on the side of the building at the sides of her head.

She shrieked in surprise. "What are you doing?"

"Taking what's mine." He captured her open mouth with his lips.

She gasped, losing her breath. The hardness with which he kissed her eased into softness and exploration. She fisted his shirt in her hands, and kissed him back.

The first swipe of his tongue weakened her legs. He pressed her against the wall, holding her up. His thigh thrust against her pelvic bone, sending pleasurable pressure scattering throughout her body. She moaned and deepened the kiss, wanting more.

Gary's body shifted down and back up, rubbing against her. She squirmed, pressing closer, loving the heat of his mouth. The impatience in his kiss. The excitement of him giving her everything she wanted without any thought, and—

He pulled his mouth away, staring down into her eyes. Anguish and confusion etched across his forehead. "We can't do this," he whispered, breathing hard. "But hell if I can take seeing you touch other men when I want your hands on me, your body against me, and your mouth on mine."

She nodded, frantic for him to understand they could and should, and she wanted and needed him.

"Not here." He glanced around. "Someone is going to see us."

He looked back to her. At the same time, they both said, "Home."

She hustled along with him to the car. He squealed out of the parking lot as he drove and passed the lot attendant at the exit gate. She latched her seatbelt by the time they hit the interstate. Excitement, anxiety, lust, and impatience swirled inside of her, making her pant and clutch at his arm as he drove.

Gary had finally come to his senses. They could work their relationship out later. Right now, she was going to go home with him, and whatever happened next, she'd accept everything he gave her.

He barely pulled into the garage, and he was hitting the remote to close the door, and ushering her through the condominium. Her shirt came off in the kitchen. His shoes were kicked to the corner of the living room. She held on to him with one hand, and hopped along beside him, dragging her pants off in the hallway.

At the bedroom door, he picked her up and sailed with her to the bed, cushioning their fall, keeping his weight off her. He gazed down into her eyes. "Tell me now if you've changed your mind. There's no going back once I'm sunk deep inside of you, Ang. I'll never let you go once I have all of you."

She warmed, stroking his cheek. "I'm begging you not to let me go."

"Honey…" He laid his forehead against hers. "This screws up your whole life."

She smiled, because for how much she loved her career and needed stability in her life, everything paled to how much Gary gave her by being beside her, letting her in his bed, and admitting that he had loved her longer than she even thought possible.

"The only thing you're screwing is me." She laughed softly, wrapping her legs around his thighs. "Don't make me wait any longer."

He nodded and kissed her quickly, before scrambling off the bed, disappearing into the bathroom and returning with a condom. She propped herself on her elbows, watching as he rolled the protection along his hard length. She inhaled a shuddering breath, wondering if she was even prepared for the size of her defensive lineman.

"It'll be fine." He moved over her, laying her back.

She sighed, relaxing. "You read minds now, huh?"

"Only yours and I want to make sure you don't take twenty minutes chitchatting about what we're going to do." He kissed her neck. "This is it, honey. Me and you."

"I wasn't going to talk," she murmured, trailing her hands up his arms and over his broad shoulders. "You won't even hear a word from me."

He shifted lower, unclasping the clip in the front of her bra and settling his mouth around her nipple, drawing the bundle of nerves deep in his mouth. She moaned, arching off the bed.

"That feels…God, so good." She dug her fingers in his hair.

While he concentrating on her breasts with his mouth, Gary pulled down her panties. She lifted her hips and kicked the offending material away. Bare and exposed, she trembled as a thrill went through her.

This wasn't anyone. Gary wasn't even her boyfriend. They'd never dated. Yet, she'd slept with him more often than she had any old boyfriend, and she'd told him more secrets than she told Jules. He slipped his hand between her legs, stroking her wetness, finding the spot that had her head coming off the mattress, and then falling back in delight.

She could worry about tomorrow later, but because everything they were doing and going to do felt right, she put her trust in the fact that whatever happened afterward, it'd be worth it.

"Gary," she said, writhing underneath him. "I need you—" she gasped as heat flooded her body "—inside me."

"Not yet." He kissed his way over her ribs, her stomach, her mound, and dipped his head.

Shock, quickly replaced with the most wonderful caress in the world, consumed her. She clutched at the comforter as his mouth, his tongue, his lips loved her. "I c-can't believe you're doing this."

He swiped his tongue, barely hitting her clitoris, but sending her higher. She panted. Her muscles strained, relaxed, and then spasmed in pleasure, unable to make their mind up whether to let her explode or to ground her to the moment.

"Oh, oh…" She squeezed her eyes as pleasure vibrated inside of her. "Right there. Right there. Gary…Right. There."

He eased back, blowing warm air over her sensitive sex. She dug her heels into the bed and bounced her hips.

"Don't stop. Not now. Go back to—"

His mouthed settled on her.

"Oh, thank God," she screamed, laughter bubbling out of her. "That feels…yes, perfect."

A nip, lick, roll between his lips, and she had no idea what she was saying, because her body convulsed on its own. Her knees came up to her chest on their own and she leaned to the side. Too sensitive to take anymore, she lay there catching her breath.

Gary moved up her body, and smiled down at her. "Finally, I've figured out a way to make you stop talking."

"I-I…" She inhaled deeply, melting again at the supreme confidence on his face. "I got nothing."

"I think you have one more." He lifted her leg to his side, and situated himself between her legs.

"Oh, God. I can't." She peered up at him. "I've never…I'm too worn out."

"I'm about to prove you wrong." He slid his hand between her legs, and fingered her wetness. She quivered under his touch, her body waking from her orgasm.

"This can't be happening," she whispered in a heavy voice.

"It's happening. You're tight, honey." He held himself and rubbed the end of his hardness along her sex.

She lifted her hips, ready for him. "It's okay. It'll be perfect. Please."

He lowered himself to his elbows, looked into her eyes, and whispered, "Yeah."

Inch by inch, he stretched her. She bit her lip on a mew of urgent need, and he gave her more instantly.

"Jesus," he said on an exhale.

She looked at him and wrapped her arms around his neck. Her hands shook and she lost concentration as he moved inside of her.

He held her eyes, and her sex squeezed him in response. His eyes warmed and his hips bucked. Never before had so much power built inside of her at the knowledge that he was reacting to what she could give him.

"I don't think I can do slow." She bucked underneath him.

"Honey," he muttered. "I've wanted you too long. I'll finish before I start and I'm taking you with me."

Then he did as he promised, moving her, stroking her, filling her. Her eyes closed from the sheer beauty, and she had to force them open because she wanted to experience it all.

Her core coiled tighter. She reached for what she knew was right there out of her reach, but pulled back because she never wanted it to end. Gary brought his mouth down and moaned against her lips, riding her harder. That was all she needed.

She drove her hips up, grinding against him, and she cried out as her world exploded for the second time. Gary trembled on top of her, going down on his elbows and rolling to the side with her, not letting her go. She laid her head against his chest, breathing hard, dizzy, and unsure if she was sleeping or awake.

She'd just made love to Gary Satchel, and it was way better than she could have ever imagined.

Chapter Fourteen

After making love and finally pulling themselves out of the bedroom, Angie's shoe tapped against the hardwood floor in the living room. Gary leaned back on the couch and clasped his hands behind his head. He hoped his relaxed pose hid the worry he tried so hard to hide.

He'd finally done it. He'd slept with the woman of his dreams, he'd sealed his heart, he'd stamped his woman with a tattoo across her ass and claimed her. His chest warmed and he wanted to throw back his head and laugh himself insane. He finally had everything he'd ever wanted, and despite his life spiraling out of control, a huge part of him wanted to celebrate.

Making love to Angie was better than he'd imagined all these years. He no longer believed he was falling in love with her, he was positive he loved her. Two people couldn't have that kind of reaction to each other and claim it was anything short of destiny.

He only wished someone would tell him what he was supposed to do next.

"We'll explain what happened," Angie said.

He shook his head. "Rules are rules. They don't give a damn that our feelings are real or that we've known each other forever. You're an employee, I'm a player, and the two don't mix. So far, they haven't found out you're staying with me, but someone is going to notice you get in my car after every practice. It's only a matter of time."

"It's unfair." She crossed her arms and paced in front of him. "There's got to be a way around everything."

"We'll wait until the season is over, and then decide how we'll approach everyone. Your contract must be renewed every year, right?"

She shook her head. "Two years. I took a hundred dollars a month cut to guarantee two years, thinking I was doing the right thing to secure employment."

"Ang…" He closed his eyes a moment, thinking twenty-four months of hiding their relationship—or worse, not seeing her—would kill him.

"Sorry." She walked into the kitchen, removed a pop from the fridge, and returned to the living room. "I didn't know at the time that we'd get together or—"

"I know." He leaned forward and put his elbows on his knees. "We'll play it cool. When you're around the team, you don't look at me, speak to me, or touch me."

"That sucks." She approached him until he leaned back, and then she climbed up on his lap. "What about riding together to practice and later to the stadium or the airport?"

"We'll stick with the story that you're a family friend who is staying with me until a condominium opens up near me. That's what you wrote on your employment paperwork. The HR department probably won't question it, and the players will never find out." He put his hands on her hips and dragged her forward.

She held her can up in the air to keep from spilling her pop. "No, I'm an awful liar. All they have to do is ask me, and they'll know we're having sex."

"Okay, we won't say anything. We'll evade the questions."

She perked up. "I still have my car in storage. We can go separately to practice. They'll never know where I go when I leave."

He grinned, leaning forward to nuzzle her neck. "Perfect."

"We'll keep it a secret." She nudged him, and he pulled away. "This could be fun. They say the thing that attracts people to having an affair is hiding their secrets. It's the thrill and mystery of it all. Only we'll be the only ones who know we're getting hot and sweaty when alone."

He fell back against the couch and laughed. "Shit. Only you would go there."

"Well, it is kind of cool. Once we tell everyone, and Drew knows…"

He groaned and grabbed her under her arms and set her off his lap. "Fuck. I need to call Drew."

How could he have forgotten? The one thing that had kept him from going anywhere with Angie was the fact that he was best friends with Drew. "He better answer his damn phone today."

"Wait!" She scrambled to her feet. "You can't tell him."

"Why not?" He held his cell in his hand. "I'm not keeping it from him."

"Because I don't want him to know." Angie sucked in her bottom lip. "Not yet."

His chest tightened and he dropped his arm. "What aren't you telling me?"

She shook her head. "Nothing. I just want to wait."

"Two days." He pointed at her. "That's all I'm giving you. We'll take the two days we have off, and decide how we'll approach Drew."

She nodded. "Yeah. That's good."

"This is a bad idea," he mumbled. "I don't know what the hell I'm doing."

Angie gasped, and the hurt in her eyes tore at his heart. He moved toward her when the doorbell rang. He looked between her and the door, knowing he had to explain how he was feeling.

"You regret last night? This morning? All week?" She spoke low, angry, and hurt.

"Yes…no." He growled and looked at the ceiling in despair. "We'll talk as soon as I find out who in the hell is at the door and send them away."

Everything between them was going too fast, despite him wanting her for years. He couldn't forget who he was and where their careers were going. She deserved someone who would be there for her all the time. Someone stable and family oriented. Not some playboy football player who came from a bad background who didn't have the balls to take their relationship public.

He stalked to the door. Yeah, when he thought about having sex with her, he regretted it, because of the secrets she'd created to keep their relationship hidden. The secrecy, the lies, the hiding… none of that she deserved, and he had taken her there when he'd decided to give up and sleep with her. He was the one responsible for fucking up her life, and they weren't even truly together yet.

He yanked the door open. "What?" he snapped.

"Hello to you too." Bruce smacked the back of his hand against Gary's chest. "I thought we were meeting downtown for lunch."

Bruce, world champion bass fisherman, was one of his best friends. He hadn't seen him since they got together in Cottage Grove a few months ago.

"Shit. I forgot you were flying in today." Gary stepped back. "Come in. I can grab you a beer at least."

Bruce walked into the condominium and stopped at the sight of Angie standing in the middle of the room with her arms crossed. "Hey, I'm sorry. I had no idea Satchel had company. I'll stop by next time I'm in town."

He slapped Bruce on the back. "It's just Angie, Drew's sister."

"Angie?" Bruce moved forward and held out his hand. "I think we met once before, right?"

Angie flashed a look at Gary, and turned to Bruce for the handshake. "Yes. At one of the clubs…I think the Blue Indigos were playing that night."

"That's right." Bruce's gaze lowered and took in Angie.

Gary cleared his throat and walked into the room. He handed a beer to Bruce. "Sit."

Angie pointed to the hallway. "I'm going to change and go out. Have a nice visit."

Gary sidestepped toward her. "Where are you going?"

"Out." She nailed him with a look, spun on her heels, and walked out of the room.

He ran his hands through his hair, and stared after her. She had a right to be upset. What they were doing sent both their lives into a tiebreaker, and he'd fumbled the ball.

"Yo, I'll leave…" Bruce set down his beer.

Gary turned around and shook his head. "Nah, stay."

They both sat down, Bruce on the couch, Gary on the chair, and neither one said anything. Gary picked at the knee of his jeans. He should go talk to Angie. She had to understand they were making a mistake.

"Woman trouble?" Bruce pulled from the bottle. "I'm sorry for interrupting. I should've called on my way over here."

"It's fine. You're fine." Gary grimaced. "I'm the one that's a mess. I don't know what the hell I'm doing."

Angie stepped into the living room, gazed at both of them, and said her goodbye to Bruce, ignoring him completely. She quietly closed the door on her way out. Gary winced, feeling the click of the door as if he'd taken a head-on tackle. He would've preferred her to slam her way out, yell at him, tell him to go to hell.

A quiet Angie scared him.

"You want to talk?" Bruce finished off his drink.

Did he? Could he? He sighed. Bruce was part of Gary's group of pro athlete friends—probably the only people in the world who would understand his predicament. Grayson Schyler was already married with a kid, Dominic Chekovsky was married and playing hockey in San Jose, Juan Santiago—hell, he never left his wife's side long enough to have a decent talk anymore. Crista was…

"What's Crista doing lately?" he said.

"Taking some R and R from the Ironman, but she's still teaching her exercise class on the big island." Bruce chuckled. "She called up to bitch me out a few days ago. Supposedly, she heard through the grapevine that I was seeing Barbara Delaney."

"The actress?" He whistled at Bruce's nod.

Bruce shook his head. "It isn't true, but I let Crista go on believing the rumor. I figure in a few days she'll fly over and explain to me how stupid I am. I'll let her stew, just so I can hold this against her."

"Cruel," he muttered. "You two have a messed up friendship."

Gary gazed at the closed door. Bruce at least had a friendship with Crista, and could withstand Crista's temper. Angie had the ability to crush him.

"Hey, man, talk to me. You look like you're in thick with it." Bruce stretched his legs out and leaned back on the sofa.

"This goes no further than this room." He waited until Bruce nodded and then confessed. "I slept with Angie."

Bruce smiled. "She's hot."

"She's Drew's sister. Fuck, she's practically family…the only family I've claimed and cared about." Gary ran his tongue over his teeth. "Drew doesn't know, and if anyone on the team finds out, Angie will lose her job. She's working as the massage therapist under the physical trainer now."

"Hang on. Did you screw up because you crossed the line and you're playing her?" Bruce rubbed his hands along his thighs. "I've never known you to let yourself go and have a good time. You've always kept women at a distance, and stayed out of long-term relationships. Man…if you're leading her on, I can't blame you for being worried. She doesn't look like your typical fangirl."

"She's not." He stood. "And our relationship isn't like that."

"Then tell me how it is, so I can understand."

Gary walked over to the window, opened the drapes, and then leaned against the windowsill. Nobody would understand, because he'd refused to allow anyone close to him. Even his best friends only knew what he wanted them to see.

"I'll figure it out on my own," he said.

"You sure?" Bruce asked.

He nodded. "Yeah."

His feelings toward Angie were his, and only his. He didn't want to share. He couldn't. Because what he held in his heart was the one wonderful thing in his life that was given freely, and she'd never asked anything in return from him. "I'll handle things."

Chapter Fifteen

Angie parked her Chevy in the driveway and shut off the engine. Three hours after leaving Gary's condominium, she no longer wanted to cry over the lackluster way Gary talked about her toward Bruce and his reluctance to move forward with a relationship. She wanted to kick him in the nuts.

She slammed the door on her way out, and marched up to the front door. Refusing to use her key, she pounded on the wood. If he wanted to treat her like a stranger after taking her to bed, she'd treat him the same.

The door opened, and Gary leaned against the doorframe. He did a full body scan, returning to her eyes, and his jaw twitched in amusement. Unprepared for his change in mood, she scoffed and stared at him in disbelief.

He wasn't worried. Hell, he was probably enjoying the freedom of having his place to himself for the last few hours. She shook her head, nailing him with a shoulder to his ribs as she swept past him. Fine. If he wanted to sit back and laugh at her, he could do it alone.

She marched to the spare bedroom and slammed the door. Too ticked off to sit, she paced. She'd expected him to apologize at the least. At the most, grovel. He'd treated her horribly and embarrassed her in front of Bruce. He'd denied any relationship with her in front of one of his friends.

Not one of the players on his team or a coach or one of his neighbors, but one of his good friends who she knew he hung around with in his free time. Someone they both knew, and someone who wouldn't tell anyone their secret.

The door opened. Gary filled the room.

"Get out," she said.

"We need to talk." He moved inside. "I get that I handled this afternoon badly when Bruce stopped by."

"You think?" She rolled her eyes. "You might as well have stamped my forehead with the word 'Done,' and high-fived Bruce while I was in the room."

"Done?" He rubbed his jaw.

"We slept together, Gary. Bruce could see that. Anyone who came in would've known I was sitting on your lap seconds before the door opened." She glanced down at the front of his jeans. "You're not exactly little."

He chuckled. She glared. His amusement grew, and he tilted his head back and barked out a laugh before doubling over and grabbing his thighs, trying to stifle his laughter and failing. She snatched a pillow off the bed and stomped over to him, hitting him over the head.

He laughed harder.

Liking the relaxed Gary she was used to, she pummeled him harder to keep from letting him off the hook. He put up his hands, and she dodged to the side, changing hit zones.

"You're an idiot." She lifted the pillow over her head.

He tackled her around the waist, picking her up and falling with her toward the bed. She landed on a scream, kicking out her legs. His weight kept her pinned to the mattress.

"Get. Off." She shoved at his chest.

He held himself above her and grinned down at her. "Kiss me."

"Get real." She heaved her body, but all she accomplished was getting her legs out from under him.

He slid between her thighs. She stilled. His hardness pressed against her. "Seriously? Arguing makes you hard? That's sick, Satchel."

He lowered his head and put his mouth below her ear. "You do that, honey. Whether you're sleeping, laughing, or hitting me with a pillow."

Okay, that was nice. Her midsection pulsed and she warmed.

"I'm sorry," he whispered. "I was rude earlier."

"Yes. You were." She swallowed, trying hard to ignore the way his body pressed into her in all the right places.

"The thing is, Ang, it's going to be harder than hell to keep this secret, and I think we need to cool down. Think about this some more." He lifted off her.

All the heat disappeared, and his words shocked her into staying quiet. The serious tone scared her. He'd once again gone from hot to cold, and she had no idea why.

"I need to know what you expect of me." He grabbed her hand and pulled her into a sitting position. "What do you see happening between us?"

"What do you mean?" She straightened her shirt and glanced at him. "We're together. You said you've always loved me, and I was more than clear that what I feel for you goes beyond friendship. I want you in my life. I don't want to lose you."

Gary leaned forward, taking her hand with him. She gazed down as he cupped her fingers between both his hands. "There's a difference between wanting me and loving me, honey," he said, quietly.

"I know that." She laid her head on his arm. "I do love you. I have forever. You know that."

"It's not the same." He leaned over and put his head on top of hers. "I know you love me as a friend. You care about my wellbeing, my happiness, my success. This is different. It's a whole different emotion because we've slept together."

She shook her head. "No, it's not. It's only better because we know each other that way. Don't you see what's happening? We're together."

"For how long?" he asked.

She pulled her hand away. "I just told you, we're together now."

"What, Ang? What comes next? Do you move in with me permanently? Do we get engaged? What about marriage? Kids?" He stood and stared down at her. "I'm not ready for those things, and I'm not sure I ever will be. I won't make the same mistake as my parents or bring any child into a life that could blow up on them in a year, five years, ten years."

"You're overthinking this. Nobody makes these kinds of decisions after sleeping with someone for the first time or when a relationship is fresh and new," she whispered, her heart breaking.

He walked to the door. Without turning around, he replied, "I do, honey. I'm not willing to throw away our friendship or my friendship with Drew to play with your heart or mine. I respect you too much, and until I know without a doubt that I can love you the way you deserve, I think we need to stop."

"Stop?" She blinked furiously to clear the moisture out of her vision.

"We'll go back to being roommates for the time being." He glanced over his shoulder. "I'm sorry. Damn sorry, honey. I didn't set out to play with you."

He walked out of the room, leaving the door wide open. She stared out into the hallway, willing him to come back and explain to her what just happened between them.

She couldn't lose him from her life. Her feelings had changed fast from friends to lovers, but she'd learned long ago she had to act before anything happened to ruin everything.

She jumped off the bed, and hurried down the hall. Gary sat in the living room, his head leaned back, his eyes closed, listening to his music, oblivious to her in the room. She reached over him and pushed the button on his MP3, shutting off his music.

"What if something happens to one of us?" Her voice raised with each word. "What then? Are you going to regret stopping what we have together? You can feel it—I know you can." She sucked air in on a sob. "Don't lie to me and tell me there's nothing between us, because I know it's real. I'll tell you every day how I feel, and I'll show you in every way I know possible how much I appreciate you in my life, but please don't cut me off and put me out of your life before you give us a chance. I don't want to lose another person I love."

She inhaled swiftly, pressing her hand against her chest. Panic swept through her, squeezing the air out of her lungs, and darkened the edges of her vision. She pulled too little air in through her opened mouth, struggling to fill her lungs.

"Shit." Gary leapt to his feet and gathered her in his arms, guiding her to the couch and setting her down. "Breathe, honey."

She shook her head. "I-I can't. You h-have to answer me."

"Later, I promise. Right now, you need to calm down." He gathered her hair off her face and held it bunched in his hand behind her neck. "Breathe slowly. In. Out."

She squeezed her eyes shut and listened to his voice. Why was this happening now?

"Ang, listen to me, honey. Just lean on me, and keep breathing." Gary pulled her closer. "I got you. I'm right here."

She sucked in air and nodded. The pressure eased, and she inhaled another shuddering breath, relief coming fast and the ache in her head loosening its ugly grip. She blinked her eyes open and pulled away, taking another breath to test herself.

"I'm okay now," she said.

He rubbed her back and she concentrated on inhaling, exhaling, and pushing all her thoughts out of her head. Embarrassed to have lost it in front of him, and having never experienced the sensations of not being able to breathe when she was awake, she sat weak and rejected beside him.

"I'm sorry," she whispered, rubbing her forehead. "I don't know what came over me."

"Ang, I think—"

"You know what?" She pressed her hands against her thighs and heaved herself to her feet, swaying on her feet. "I'll leave you alone. I think I'll just take it easy…maybe nap."

He wrapped his fingers around her wrist and pulled her back, catching her before she landed on the couch, and shifted her to his lap. "How long have you had panic attacks?"

"What?" She shook her head. "I don't…"

"I've seen grown men have them before a game or when they reach exhaustion. It's not something to be embarrassed about." Gary smoothed her head off her cheek. "You had one the other night while you were sleeping too."

"I'd like to lie down," she said.

"You're not leaving my sight until you tell me what's going on with you." He kept her on his lap. "You were upset about losing me, and talking about death again."

"Please," she said, hating the whine in her voice.

Gary's chest inflated and he slowly let out his breath. "Damn. I should've known."

"It was a long time ago," she whispered.

"I know. But she was your mom," he said. "You were with her."

She had been the only one with her mom when she'd died at home. The hair at the back of her neck tickled, and she shivered. That night, Drew and Gary had left to go to a party, and she'd told them it was okay because she was going to stay up and watch television. She'd planned to sit in her mom's bedroom in case she needed anything. Her days were numbered, they all knew that, but that day was one of her mom's better ones and she thought she'd be fine alone. Her mom had slept peacefully for a couple hours.

After the movie on television ended, she'd crawled in bed with Mom to watch the late show while she waited for the boys.

She leaned her head against Gary and closed her eyes.

She'd fallen asleep. Sometime later, whether she sensed something wrong in the room or the boys shut the door as they came in—something woke her up, and her mom wasn't breathing.

Gary and Drew had come in when she was trying to give her mom CPR. She'd had no idea how to do it right, but only knew she had to try. She hadn't been ready to lose her mom.

"That's why you sleep with me," Gary whispered.

"Yeah," she whispered back. "I hate being alone—in my head, I hate being alone. I know I'm being stupid."

"No, you're not." He sighed deeply. "You're not going to lose me. I'm right here. We'll keep things secret for however long we can, and slow down. We'll just…slow down."

She swallowed hard. "Okay," she whispered. "Thank you."

"But we need to tell Drew," he said.

She thought of the extra stress that'd add to their relationship, the questions her brother would ask, and the position he'd put Gary in when he found out they'd kept the news from him. "That can wait."

"It's the only way I'll go forward, Ang. Drew means too much to me. You mean too much," he said.

His arms pulled her snug against him. She held on, afraid she'd lose him too. Whether her fear of losing another person she loved was irrational, her anxiety over losing Gary was real. With the Seahawks threatening her, and not knowing how her brother would act, they were living on borrowed time.

Chapter Sixteen

Fist to the ground, knees bent, head up, Gary was out for blood. Last down in the scrimmage, and he was done. Completely—fucking—done.

"Angie's a nice piece of ass. I wouldn't mind tappin' that." Cormac grinned.

The whistle blew. Gary charged straight for Cormac. Tackling him low, he took the man down.

"Oomph." Cormac groaned. "Shit, man, save it for our first game."

Gary brought his head back and swiftly helmet butted the other player. "Open your mouth again about Ms. Swanson, and I'll do more than knock the wind out of your stupid ass."

He pushed off Cormac and got to his feet, glaring over his shoulder at the fallen player as he walked away. Two weeks of hiding his relationship with Angie from the team, and he wondered if he was insane to even think he'd be able to hide his feelings any longer when he had to listen to them talk about her all the time. At home, everything was good. They'd grown closer, but both of them were making an effort to slow things down between them. Angie understood he couldn't give her much of a future, except to always be there for her, for however long they both were happy with the arrangement.

When she was around, he could ignore the fact that a woman like her who valued commitment, family, and security would soon ask him for more than he could give. Nobody had ever asked him for anything. The closest he'd come to committing himself to something was signing a football contract. Even that didn't last forever.

He wasn't sure he had the skills to make a serious relationship. Living in foster care growing up, he'd always known he'd be leaving and the people in his life weren't permanent. He had an idea of what family was like from the Swansons, but what if he failed when things became tough?

Right now, she was satisfied. He knew that, because she used every chance to tell him, like she promised she'd do.

Over breakfast, she'd touch him. When they went out for their morning run, she stayed silent, sharing in their solitary run, but pushing him to go a longer distance, and he was running farther. At night, she crawled into his bed.

There were no more night terrors.

He'd figured out if he wore her out by making love to her, she slept like a baby. Warmth filled his chest. Except last night, she'd taken the offense position, and blew his game plan, and surprised the hell out of him.

She'd shown up naked in his room, and before he knew it, she was riding the hell out of him. How was he supposed to turn down that?

He looped into a jog, anxious to go home. He and Angie both had the next two days off. Drew was coming over later today. They'd agreed that a face-to-face talk would work better to break the news than telling him over the phone. He expected Drew to punch his face. Angie expected a happy family reunion.

He pushed through the locker room doors and stopped. Tension stole his next breath.

Moans echoed in the tiled room. He clenched his teeth, and pushed his way inside. That made three players on the team that turned into total moaners at the touch of Angie's hands.

He stripped out of his clothes without looking in the back of the room at Angie while she worked on one of the players. He'd get his own massage at home. And, yes, he'd moan just as loud or even louder.

"Satchel. Office." Coach waved him over from the doorway.

He lifted his chin in answer, grabbing a towel to wrap around his waist. The other guys jeered. It was never a good sign to be called out, and he'd never been reprimanded before. But he deserved whatever Coach had to say. His aggression on the field and his bitchy attitude toward the others was not how a Seahawks player behaved.

At the office door, he glanced at Angie. She'd stilled with her hands above Johnson. Guilt riddled her features.

Shit.

Cormac wouldn't have told anyone of their altercation on the field. Scuffles and words were thrown around all the time. Life stresses, game pressure, and exhaustion got the better of all of them. But the worry on Angie's face concerned him. They both knew anyone watching them could get there was more going on between them.

"Close the door and have a seat," Coach said, tossing his clipboard on the desk.

Gary sat, tucking the end of the towel at his hip and leaning forward. "Problem, Coach?"

"You tell me." Coach leaned forward and propped his elbows on the desk. "Is Angie Swanson living with you?"

"Yes, sir." He nodded, looking him in the eye. The coach had no reason to be suspicious. Angie had put his address on her employee paperwork and let it drop that Gary was a family friend. They'd been careful.

Coach's lips tightened over his teeth and he broke his gaze and looked at the desk. "What kind of relationship would you say you have with Ms. Swanson?"

"A long term relationship, sir," he said.

Coach whipped his gaze back to him. "Think carefully before you answer, son. You and I both know what having a relationship with Ms. Swanson means for you and her."

"Yes, sir, and I know what it'll do to her career with the Seahawks if rumors go further than this room." Gary remained calmed. "I've known her and her family since I was thirteen years old. Her family practically raised me. Her brother, Drew, is my best friend. As a matter of fact, I'm the one who recommended her for the job with the team. I know exactly what our relationship is. I picked her up at her brother's house in Deadhorse, Oregon, and brought her back to the city to fulfill her job. She's staying with me until she finds an apartment. Because I promised her brother I would look out for her, it's taking longer to find a place that is safe enough for her on short notice. We'll both be traveling when the games start, and be away from home for most of the time. We figured it would be best to keep on with what we've set up… in which her brother is thankful for, considering we're all family."

Coach's eyes narrowed and he studied Gary. "Take this as a warning that if I hear of anything going on between you two, even a fucking kiss on the cheek, I'll have to report you."

He stood and nodded. "Understood."

Beating his escape, he walked out of the office and straight into the showers. He closed his eyes, letting the water roll down him. He hadn't lied.

He'd left certain parts out, but the coach wasn't asking for a full confession. Everything he said was true. They'd known each other forever and their history was ingrained in him as much as any family has a bond that doesn't break when one of the members need some extra help or a spare bedroom.

He opened his eyes, and looked straight out at Angie. She'd finished her massage and was bent over, putting her bag away. The price of the fine he'd pay for breaking the rules had no stigma attached. Players screwed up all the time. They paid their way out of trouble, and the penalty wouldn't put a dent in his bank account.

Besides, no one wanted to kick a valuable player off the team, especially in a year where the Seahawks were expected to go all the way to the Super Bowl. Angie's job, on the other hand, was expendable.

Maybe once Drew arrived, he'd talk some sense into both of them. If anyone knew how important Angie's job was, Drew did. He'd lived with her, and put up with the stress of her surviving on unemployment and the feeling of uselessness she battled. Not to mention the boredom. No, Angie needed this job.

He dried off, dressed in his street clothes, ignoring the other players' questioning looks about what he was called out for, and went about gathering his things. It wasn't anyone's business what went on in his life as long as he played his best.

Even after taking the time to meet with Coach, he beat the other players out of the locker room, which was becoming a habit. He was able to make it out to his car and leave before Angie left. To everyone else, it looked like they went their separate ways.

He cranked the radio and rolled down the window. The talk that would come when Angie arrived home was not something he looked forward to. She lived life from her heart, and her actions came from caring, showing, loving. This time, she'd have to use her head, and be smart, thinking of her career first. It was time to face reality, and stop pretending that they could continue living the way they were in secret.

What kind of man would he be if he let her ruin her life? The position with the Seahawks would set her up for life. If she wanted to quit after her two years were up, she'd have instant success if she wanted to go out on her own and start her own spa or run a business with private clientele. Hell, half the players had experienced her hands, and would love to continue her treatment long after she moved on in her career.

Maybe he'd made the wrong decision, encouraging her by admitting they could make this work. He'd agreed to keep everything secret. That was what he wanted and dreamed about. He didn't want to change a damn thing, but there was more going on than just their personal life. He'd put her in the position of worrying about her job, and that sat wrong with him.

He pulled up to the gate, pushed a few buttons, and waited for the iron fence to open. He drove home.

In his driveway sat a Dodge Charger. He shut off the radio and looked in his rearview mirror for Angie's car. What the hell was Drew doing here already?

He wasn't due until closer to dinnertime. Gary parked out on the street, leaving the extra space in the driveway for Angie when she arrived.

Drew held up his hand and pushed off the fender of his car, walking to meet Gary halfway in the driveway. Without a word, he grabbed Drew into a hug and thumped his back.

"Shit, Satchel, ease up, big guy." Drew punched him on the shoulder, stumbling backward.

"You're early." He motioned with his head. "Come on in. Angie should be pulling in at any time. Practice only ended an hour ago. I wasn't expecting you this early."

"I left earlier than I planned. I hope you have a beer. It was a hell of a long drive." Drew threw him a grin.

He unlocked the door. "Go ahead and grab one. I'll be right back."

Gary searched the living room for anything that would hint at his and Ang's relationship. A pair of panties, the scarf he'd used to keep her hands off him, a box of condoms. Seeing nothing incriminating, he hurried to the bedrooms and shut both doors. Angie never made the bed, and if Drew looked, he'd see the bed in the spare room was made and un-slept in. His room looked like a bomb exploded. Angie had more clothes than ten women put together, and believed in spreading each piece over every surface in the room for easy pickings in the mornings.

Shutting the door, he quickly headed back to the living room. Angie was due any time, and he wanted to talk to Drew by himself. He owed him that much.

"Hey." Gary pulled up a chair at the dinette off the kitchen. "I need to talk to you, and it can't wait."

"Dammit. I knew something was wrong with Angie. Between her phone calls and you going off the deep end about following rules…" Drew rubbed his hands over his face. "Just tell me. Did she lose the job?"

Gary sighed and looked up at the ceiling for understanding before meeting Drew's eyes. "We're sleeping together."

Drew stood without saying anything or giving him a hint of what he was thinking. Gary watched him walk a few paces away before turning around, and then Drew said, "I did not need to know that."

"I know, man." Gary laid his hand flat to the table. "It wasn't something that happened out of the blue for me. I've wanted her for years, but never made the moves on her because she was your sister."

Drew held up his hand. "Stop. Really."

"Drew, you have to understand—"

"No, really, I don't. It's none of my business what you two—" Drew shuddered. "Jesus, bro, my sister?"

The revulsion was apparent on Drew's face, the way he avoided Gary's gaze. His chest tightened. The last thing he wanted was Drew mad at him or Angie.

Gary nodded. "I know, but I swear I'm not trying to hurt her."

Drew sat back down and blew out his breath. Gary flexed his fingers, wishing he had an easy answer for Drew.

"This is all new for her. She had no idea I felt more than friendship for her, and surprised me by putting the moves on me," he said, lifting his hands.

Drew pinned him with a look. "Okay, that's going too far."

"Sorry. That's not what I meant. This is my fault, not hers." Gary rubbed his hand over his lower face. "That's why we had you come over. We wanted you to know, but there's more going on that you need to find out. I need your help."

"For what? It looks like you've created your own problem, you can find your way out…and if you hurt my sister, I'll hurt you." Drew's breath came fast and he shook his head.

Gary wished he could explain better to put Drew at ease. But he understood Drew's frustration, and that's why he'd kept his hands off Angie for years.

"I'd expect you to. I'm not trying to hurt her, but if she and I keep going at it during the season, she could end up losing her job. She's under contract. So am I. We can't have a personal relationship beyond working together," he said. "I've told her we have to wait, but she wants to keep it secret, and I'm finding it harder than anything I've ever done to stay away from her."

The door swung open. Gary turned and hated that he'd broken his word and told Drew first. Maybe now Angie would realize how serious he was.

"Drew." Angie dropped her bag and ran across the room, throwing herself into Drew's arms. "You're early."

"Yeah." Drew kissed her cheek. "Been catching up with Gary. So, you're sleeping with my best friend."

Angled bugged her eyes out at Gary. "Um, surprise."

Gary stood. "Angie, listen to—"

A knock came at the door. Gary cussed. "I'll get it."

The last thing he needed was company coming during what he knew would be a heated discussion. Drew was only staying through the evening, and then heading back to Deadhorse. That gave them all little time to straighten out two lives.

He opened the door and clenched his teeth.

An older version of Drew stood in front of him. Except, Angie and Drew's father had less hair on his head, wore glasses, and his middle protruded more since the last time Gary had seen him.

"Gary." Teak held out his hand, ushering two small kids into the room.

He shook Teak's hand and sidestepped the little girl. He hadn't seen Angie's half siblings before, or the leggy red-haired woman who trailed in smiling at him.

"This is my wife, Jojo." Teak walked past him. "Hell, I didn't know we were having a family reunion."

Teak threw his arms around Drew, moved to Angie and spoke low, kissing her cheek, and then stepped over to hang his arm around his wife. Gary approached the group, thinking he'd stepped into hell.

Never a fan of Teak Swanson, he wondered how the man knew where to find his family and why he was here. From what he'd collected from Angie, Teak only showed up if he needed something.

The last thing they needed were more problems to solve.

Chapter Seventeen

Angie held her sister, Tabby, on her lap, while her brother, Tyler, sat beside her playing with her phone. She mouthed *sorry* across the room to Gary. It was true she had told her dad she'd watch the kids if he figured out where she could take them during the day while she was working. It was only for two nights, and she'd promised him she'd babysit before she'd decided not to move out of Gary's condo.

With all the chaos with their relationship, practice, and worrying about Drew's reaction, she'd forgotten to tell Gary about her agreeing to keep the kids if her dad couldn't find an ulterior plan.

Like usual, her dad half worked out a new plan. Somehow he'd found a woman who lived two condos down from Gary to babysit while Angie worked, but she still had to take care of the kids when she was home at Gary's.

"Can we go swimming?" Tyler brushed his long bangs out of his eyes.

At six years old, he took his duty as advisor and older brother seriously—often times being rude and bossy, and not taking no for an answer. Angie patted his thin leg. "We'll see."

"I don't wanna swim," whined Tabby. At four years old, she rarely wanted to do anything that might hurt, scare, or excite her.

"Let's finish talking to your parents and then we'll decide," Angie said.

Drew shook his head at Angie and frowned at Gary. "It's my sister's career," he said, picking up their conversation where they'd left off. "I'll stay in town and help her find an apartment."

For the next ten minutes, her relationship with Gary led to a debate with all her family members on how to run her life. She ignored the lot of them, because at the end of the day, it didn't matter what they thought was best for her. She wanted to stay here, and keep her relationship with Gary secret. It was a gamble she was willing to take to stay close to Gary.

"You're not helping me find a place to live." Angie smiled at Tabby and ticked her belly. "Grownups are so funny, aren't they?"

"She can stay at our house." Teak rocked back on his heels. "We'll put the kids together and she can have Tyler's room."

"I'm not moving in with you, Dad." Angie rolled her eyes. "What none of you are doing is listening to me. I hate when you do that."

"I think she's doing the right thing." Jojo wrapped her arms around Teak, and smiled at Angie.

"Thanks." Angie grinned back.

"I'll go to a hotel, while Angie stays here. We've got two weeks until the first game. After that we'll be on the road and our schedule will change again." Gary stood.

Angie set Tabby beside her and stood, blocking Gary's retreat. "You're not going anywhere."

"Ang, it's for the best." Gary looked at the others before turning his attention back to her and lowering his voice. "What kind of man would I be if I let you take the fall for me? There's nothing I can do, short of walking away from the team, which I can't do, so I'll stay at the Hyatt. A couple of the other guys stay there during the season. It's no big deal. If anyone asks me why I'm not living at home, I'll tell them I'm remodeling and it interrupts my sleep."

"No big deal? You'd be lying again." She shook her head in disbelief. "This is messed up."

Gary looked at the kids. "You need to stay here. It's better for them."

"Don't. Do. It," she whispered. "Don't."

He leaned down and kissed her forehead. "I need to."

Gary walked out of the room. She turned on everyone else. "Thanks a lot."

"Sis…" Drew approached her. "It's only until the contract is over. What Gary is saying makes sense. Your career is too important to throw it away for something so new. You'll have time afterward, when you've got two years of working with the Seahawks on your résumé and can move to a different job."

"Bullshit," she hissed, so the kids wouldn't overhear. "You're not thinking about me or Gary. You just want to solve our problem. This won't help anything."

Furious, she fought the tears that threatened to come. Not one of them understood how she was feeling. No one asked her what she wanted. No one cared. Not even Gary.

Maybe Jojo understood, but when it came to her and Drew, she stayed out of their business.

Gary was taking the easy way out, just like her father always did. She clamped her lips together. He'd told her in many ways that he wasn't cut out to be her boyfriend. Well, he proved it by caving to everyone else.

Let him run away. She wasn't going to go crawling back to him, because the man she loved was never going to leave her. Period.

"Hey, kids." Angie kneeled down in front of them. "Why don't we go swimming?"

Tyler jumped up and punched the air. "Yes!"

"No!" Tabby moved toward her and threw her arms around her neck.

Angie picked up her sister, groaning under the weight. *Geez, when did these kids grow so big?*

"How about you and me sit at the side of the pool and watch your brother swim?" she asked.

Tabby nodded against her neck. Angie turned to her dad. "Can you bring their bags in?"

Angie had Tyler dressed in his shorts and out the door in less than five minutes with strict orders that everyone needed to leave the house while she was gone. Fed up with everyone, and unable to figure out what to do about Gary, she wanted alone time to think. Alone time with two young kids in need of attention.

From the outside pool area, she kept one eye on Tyler in the shallow part of the pool and the other eye on the road that swept beside the chain-link fence. Drew left first, then her dad and his wife, and last, Gary drove off in his car.

"Angie, why you sad?" Tabby patted her cheeks, trying to pull the corners of Angie's mouth upward.

She forced a smile. "Because you've grown so big, since I saw you a few weeks ago. You're practically all grown up. Soon you're going to be a pretty young lady who is going to steal my boyfriends in a few years."

Inside, she wished Tabby were twenty years older, a sister closer to her age who would understand how much she wanted to pick up one of the lawn chairs sitting around the pool and throw it at someone. Especially if that person was named Gary and big as a house.

Instead, she was stuck stealing comfort from a four-year-old.

"You're squeezin' too tight," Tabby said.

"Sorry, sweetie." She relaxed her hold and nodded toward the pool. "Our brother is half fish, isn't he?"

Tabby giggled. "That's what Daddy says."

For the next three hours, she sat watching Tyler flip, float, and splash in the pool. Tabby fell asleep on her lap after a half hour, giving her a lot of time to think. One thing that was apparent in all her back and forth reasonings on what went wrong today was Gary had a sense of chivalry that crushed normal men.

He wanted to protect her. Fine.

He wanted to save her from having her heart broken. Fine.

He wanted to take control of their relationship. Fine.

He wanted to walk away without listening to what she wanted. Hell no.

Chapter Eighteen

Tyler ran past the coffee table, whooshing the papers Angie had spread out on the surface onto the floor. She grabbed the back of his T-shirt and hauled him back onto her lap.

"Ten minutes of remaining in one spot. That's all I ask." She kissed the side of his face, making him squirm. "Why don't you find all the pillows in the house and line them up in the hallway. Take your sister and pretend you're walking on clouds. Can you do that for me, buddy?"

He nodded and scooted away from her. "Come on, Tab. Let's go play."

Angie stuck her lower lip out and blew the stray hairs out of her vision. After spending all evening entertaining the kids, and staying up half the night with Tabby who decided she didn't like sleeping in the spare bedroom and wanted to sleep with her, she was behind on getting her reports filled out on the treatment of the players under her care. They were due tomorrow.

She crawled around the coffee table, picking up papers, trying to put them in order, when the door opened. Her heart raced.

Gary stood inside, looking more delicious than yesterday. Not that she was going to tell him that. She was still mad.

"What are you doing here?" She put the papers down and pulled herself onto the couch to find the pen she'd had in her hand a moment ago and was now missing.

"It's my home," he said.

"I know that." She shoved her fingers between the cushions and dug out the pen. "I mean, I figured you'd stay away in your hurry to get away from me. Did you forget to take everything with you to the hotel?"

Tabby shrieked, breaking the tension. Angie hurried down the hallway and came to an erupt halt. Not only had Tyler put all the pillows in the hallway, but also the towels from the bathroom, and as many clothes as he could haul by himself in five short minutes. Tabby stood there covered from head to toe with dirty clothes.

"Geez, Ty. Please tell me you're going to pick this mess up." She pulled Gary's jersey off Tabby's head, so she could breathe.

"We're trying to build a fort, and she's propping the middle up." Tyler kicked everything into a pile. "We need it bigger, but it keeps falling."

"Listen, kids. No more clothes. Play with what is out here, and then I'll give you ice cream if you build something really cool and safe. I don't want anyone suffocating. Just give me a few moments to do my job, 'kay?" She waited, and finally Tyler nodded.

She turned to go back into the living room and ran into Gary. "Sorry."

"I'll keep them out of your hair. You go work," he said.

"Are you sure?" She glanced over her shoulder. "They're a handful."

Gary studied her brother and sister. "I can do it."

"Thanks." She hurried into the other room before he could change his mind.

Her job required hands-on work, but every two weeks she filled out the progress charts for the physical therapists. For insurance reasons, they needed to keep a tight record of all treatments for the players to qualify to play and pass their physical. With the first game coming up in less than a week, it was necessary for her to do the work today.

An hour and a half later, she was finally done. She closed her eyes and rubbed her temples. A small headache grabbed hold, and she pushed herself off the floor and went in search of some aspirin in the kitchen.

After she downed the glass of water, she took out the ice cream to let it get soft enough to scoop. She owed Gary. When she'd started, she thought she'd get done faster but the coding threw her off. Most of the players were privately insured and she wasn't familiar with lingo required for the company and needed to make sure she verified each one.

Making her way down the hallway, she cocked her head, wondering what they were doing so quietly. She stepped into Gary's bedroom and peered at the multiple blankets hung around the room.

From the high bedpost to the dresser handle, and the closet door to the bathroom door. Gary had turned the bedroom into a makeshift circus tent with tunnels. She got down on her hands and knees, winding her way through the maze, over pillows, under a sheet, and squirming her way to the other side of the bed.

There she stopped, lay down on her belly, and took in the sight.

Gary lay on his back asleep. An open playbook dropped on his chest. Tyler lay beside Gary with his head on Gary's stomach, snoring softly. She swallowed hard, her attitude toward Gary softening at the sight of her man. Because any man who would let a little girl curl up under his arm and put her little cheek on his shoulder and read a football playbook to a young boy who craved male attention would always have a special place in her heart. Even when he made her mad.

Looking at the scene in front of her, she wondered why Gary believed he wasn't a good example for kids or feared he'd fail in parenting like his mother or the numerous foster parents he'd unfortunately had. Kids were simple. They required love, attention, and guidance. He exceeded the requirements.

Not once had her dad built blanket forts with her that she could remember, and she still loved him. Sure, her dad was a little flighty and irresponsible, but she'd grown up okay. Tyler and Tabby were handling life fine too, and knew how much they were loved.

Despite Gary's upbringing, he had the tools to be a terrific father. She shifted, preparing to turn around and leave them all to their nap when Gary whispered, "Hey."

"Hey, you," she whispered back. "Think you can get out of here without waking them?"

He slid his arm out from under Tabby, putting her head on a spare blanket. Then he rearranged Tyler. She turned around and crawled back through the maze, popping out at the door.

Gary followed her into the kitchen. She put away the ice cream, hoping the kids would stay asleep for a while.

"Thanks for watching them. I didn't think it would take that long." She shoved her hands in her back pockets. "That was quite the fort you built in the bedroom."

He shrugged. "When you grow up sharing a bedroom with four others, you learn how to construct ways to find privacy. I excelled at fort building as long as I had blankets and cardboard boxes, and could tie a knot."

She leaned against the counter. "You don't talk about your life with your foster family. Was it so horrible?"

"It wasn't hard or easy." He rubbed the back of his neck. "I was fed and had a place to sleep. My foster parents had anywhere from four to eight kids under their care while I stayed with them. They enjoyed the money they received from the state. I survived."

"No love," she murmured.

He grunted. "No. Which gives me nothing to go on in my own life. I don't know how to handle what is happening between us, and all I'm doing is hurting you. That's the last thing I want to happen, Ang. I want us to go back to what we had. Friendship. I'd rather have that than be kicked out of your life because I made the stupid decision to sleep with you."

"I'm going to pretend you didn't mean that the way it came out," she said.

He shook his head. "I loved having you in my bed, but I'm scared of not having you in my life as much as you are afraid of losing me…don't you see?"

She took two steps and stood in front of him. She placed her hands on his stomach. He tensed, but she refused to let him retreat. "What I see is a man who cares so much for me he's willing to make his own life hell if it means I'll be happier without him. What you're not hearing is I'm not happy without you."

"Ang…" he muttered.

"No. You've told me how you feel, and I get it. I do." She moved her hands up to his chest and leaned against him. "But you're not seeing and believing what I'm experiencing. You tell me you have no confidence in making a relationship work. I know differently, because I've had the man who stayed by my side when I needed him most. Baby, you'd sit in the hallway night after night, so I could sleep without panicking. I had no idea of your feelings back then, and you still led with your heart."

"I couldn't leave you alone," he said, cupping her face.

"I know that now." She softened. "You told me you weren't father material, and I saw proof in your bedroom that you are. I don't remember my father ever playing with me or taking the time to read a play book to me."

"I wasn't reading the plays. I made up some stupid story about bears—for Tyler—and glittery fairies for Tabby. I don't even know what fairies are." He sighed. "I just talked, that's all. I had no idea what I was doing or saying."

She nodded as he talked, blinking back the tears. "Because you led with your heart. That's what I'm telling you. You can be scared and have second guesses about what you're doing, but your heart doesn't steer you wrong. You might not have children—"

"I want kids." He pulled her tight against him and cupped her head. "Lying there playing with your little brother and sister made that dream come alive, because when I look at them, I see Tabby has your eyes, and Tyler…hell, the kid is trouble, just like you were growing up. I want to hold my little girl, and roughhouse with my son. I want to dry tears and bolster confidence, so they never doubt for one day they are worth my love."

"You can do that," she said, closing her eyes, thankful that he was finally understanding what she'd seen in him from the beginning.

"I'm scared to death I'll fail."

She pulled her head back and gazed up at him. "I am too, but when you're in my life, I can lean on you. I want you to lean on me too. Together, we'll be okay."

He sighed. "We still have the problem with your job."

"One day at a time." She stretched to her tiptoes and kissed him. "It's our business. No one needs to know and if they find out, it's okay. It's a chance I'll take."

"What happens if I'm doing the wrong thing or we screw up? I don't want you to hate me for ruining your one big chance with the Seahawks." He dropped his hands. "You know what? Never mind."

Her breath caught. "What do you mean?"

"If you can trust me, I'll trust that you're telling me the truth and this arrangement is what you want," he said.

"We'll be back together?" she asked, clasping her hands in front of her.

"Yeah, honey, we'll be back together." He hooked her neck, bringing her forward. "I need you. I want you. I love you."

She closed her eyes and kissed him. Against his lips, she whispered, "I love you too."

He palmed her ass, and deepened the kiss. The stroke of his tongue created a wave of pleasure. She'd missed him last night, and never wanted to spend another night without him.

"Beautiful," he murmured, working his way along her jaw, her neck. "Couldn't stand the hotel."

"Come home." She arched her back, her nails digging into his shoulders.

"Yeah," he said on an exhale.

His warm breath tickled her skin and she squirmed against him. "God, I want to—"

"Angie? What are you doing with Gary?" Tyler said.

She shrieked and jumped back, covering the base of her neck. Her heart beat wildly, and she looked between Tyler and Gary. Her brother looked at her curiously. Gary appeared proud of her flustered state.

"Get your sister, sport. It's time for ice cream." Gary scooted Tyler out of the room.

She rounded on Gary, smacking his arm as she opened the freezer and removed the ice cream again. Gary pinned her against the fridge, circling her waist with his arms. She softened. "Tonight, the kids are going to bed early, so you better wear them out after I load them up with ice cream."

"You'll sleep with me once we get them to bed and they're fast asleep?" he whispered, kissing her neck. "We could keep the blanket fort up, and hide away from your brother and sister."

She laughed, looking over her shoulder at him. "Is that why you built the granddaddy of all forts?"

He let her go, laughing. "You'll have to wait until tonight to find out."

Chapter Nineteen

Gary threw his helmet against the wall of the locker room, and followed Coach. The last botched tackle couldn't have come at a worse time. First game of the season was two days away.

"Got another one for you, Angie." Coach slapped down a paper onto the table.

Angie turned and gasped. Gary shrugged, winching.

"What happened?" She swiped up the paper, scanning the lines. "Sit down, but don't lie down until I loosen you up."

Coach slapped Gary's ass and left. He plunked down on the table. Unconsciously, he'd avoided having his turn with Angie. He got all the massages he wanted at home, and being around her while with the team was asking for trouble.

"Are you in much pain?" she asked when they were alone.

He shook his head. "Clipped Maloney's thigh and tweaked my left arm back. It's sorta numb right now, but nothing's torn or pulled. I know that much, so don't write that down."

"Let me do my job and make that decision." She moved around the table. "Let me help you get your pads off. Don't lift your arms. I'll cut away the shirt."

He sat motionless, letting her strip away his jersey. When the material fell away, he reached up to untie the front of his shoulder pads, and she stopped him.

"Let me," she whispered.

Angie stood between his knees, her fingers taking their sweet time. This close to her, he reacted.

"You smell good," he said.

She smiled, glancing at him. "Ah, shucks, that's what all the stinky players tell me."

"Better not be," he muttered.

She laughed softly. "Jealous?"

"From day one." He put his hands on her hips and dragged her closer.

"Gary." Her voice warned him.

He scanned the locker room and smiled. There was an hour left of practice. Unless someone had to use the john or were injured and looking for Angie, they were alone.

"Come here," he said.

"I'm right here." She spread the front of his pads and wiggled them down his arms, then paused to look at him. "What?"

"Kiss me." He held her arms, bringing her hands to the front of him. "Before someone comes in here and ruins my fantasy."

She gave him a quick peck. "Fantasy?" she said on a laugh.

"Hell, yeah." He dragged her back for a real kiss. "You. Me. The table. Maybe the shower afterward. You wearing my jersey, and nothing else…"

"Stop." She quivered. "We can't."

"What? The girl who swore to me she loved the idea of keeping us secret is too chicken to fool around behind everyone's back?" He leaned back to look her in the eyes. "Brawk…"

"I am not." She stepped away and pointed. "I think you're loose enough that we can get started on your massage. Lie down."

"No, ma'am." He grinned, sliding off the table and backing her across the room. "In all my daydreams, it was me calling the shots, not you. You wouldn't believe what I had you doing…and you loved it."

She kept retreating, staying one foot away from him. "I did?"

"Yeah." He closed the distance and took her to the wall. He pressed into her. "Of course, in my head, I wasn't wearing a damn cup in my jockstrap and covered in sweat."

She giggled as he kissed her neck. "Is that what I'm feeling?"

He grunted his answer. If he were home right now, he'd have her flat on her back and be inside of her.

But he wasn't home. He was in the locker room.

He ran his hands down the side of her, around to her ass, and lifted, ignoring the weakness in his arm. Propping his leg between her thighs, he held her higher to trace the open V of her shirt with his lips.

"Your shoulder," she panted.

"Can't feel a thing." He spoke against her skin, and she must've liked it because she shuddered.

He tugged at the bottom of her shirt, pulling it free from her pants. Her quick intake of air urged him on. He wanted nothing more than to put his mouth on her. Taste her excitement, the desire, the wicked sense of getting away with something they both know could burn them in the end.

She groaned. He swept the cup of her bra down and exposed her perky breast. His lips covered the tight peak, and he drew his tongue over it in tender licks. Her nipple tightened and he moaned when her fingers sank into his hair, holding him there.

Blindly, he sucked as if at any moment, someone would steal his chance with Angie. He couldn't get enough of her.

Her weight pressed against his thigh, and she moved her hips. He damned his pants with the thin padding, the cramped size of his athletic cup, and all the clothes Angie had on. But if he couldn't have her fully, he'd give her the next best thing.

He trailed his hand down the front of her stomach, spanning the soft curve. She sucked in her breath, and he slipped inside her jeans, and found the wetness he knew would be there. She clung to his shoulders, and he lifted his head, capturing her mouth. She rode his fingers, his leg, and he showed her with his tongue what he'd like to be doing.

Wild and crazed, she moaned. He stroked, circled, and filled her, never missing a beat. He wanted her to come fast and furious, the same way he was feeling. Raw need pushed him on. His toes dug into the soles of his cleats, and his balls ached in pleasure.

"That's it, honey." He leaned his forehead against the top of her head. "Come for me."

She nodded. Her fingernails dug into his ribs and she lifted her gaze, locking on to him. The powerful trip of having her eyes on him, trusting him, and coming undone by him almost had him losing control himself.

Then her eyelids fluttered, and her whole body shuddered. Her thighs squeezed his leg, and she sagged forward, resting on his chest as her orgasm rocked her. He slid his hand out of her jeans, lowered his leg, and held on to her.

A door swooshed in the distance. She jolted, swaying on her feet. He stepped back, keeping a hand on her back.

"Okay?" He kissed her quickly, grinning.

She pushed him away. "Go, go, go…get on the table."

He lumbered off, uncomfortable and hard as a rock. His butt hit the table at the same time John walked into the room. Gary rolled his shoulder and lifted his chin.

"How's the player?" John asked Angie.

She'd somehow grabbed a paper towel when he turned his back, and wadded it up into a ball, tossing it into the wastebasket. "Stiff."

Gary choked, and went into a fit of coughing.

Angie and John stared at him. He waved his hand and shook his head. "I'm fine…"

She'd pay for that remark when they got home. He'd take her two, three times and make her beg for mercy.

"Go ahead and suit down, go home. Ice your shoulder tonight and heat it thoroughly before the game on Sunday." John walked over and raised his arm, while prodding around on Gary's back. "You're more tense than I'd hoped after being manipulated by Angie's therapy. I'm putting you down for an appointment with the doctor, so be here an hour early pre-game."

"Shit," he muttered. "I'm fine."

John's head remained tilted toward the clipboard, but he raised his gaze. "I'll be the judge of that on Sunday."

Gary rubbed his forearm across his chin. Tomorrow, he'd take it easy, lie around, do some easy stretching, and keep himself limber. He'd be ready for the game. He was starting defense. He wouldn't let the team down.

While John conversed with Angie, Gary stripped down and walked into the showers. A full on cold shower shocked him to his senses, left his shoulder throbbing, his teeth chattering, and his dick limp.

He couldn't continue this path if he expected to play a successful season.

Chapter Twenty

Still shaken from her night terror, Angie stood in front of the window watching the sun rise over the city. She'd lain in bed until she grew too antsy and needed to get up, knowing she shouldn't bother Gary when he needed his sleep before the big game. As much as she'd tried, her mind wouldn't shut down.

Yesterday, she'd stepped over the line. What she and Gary did together in the locker room during practice was not wrong. It was right. Perfect.

But fooling everyone, especially John, who trusted her to do her job, was causing her more stress than she would have imagined. Despite her family's opinion, and Gary's determination that she fulfill all two years of her contract, she knew in her heart that what she really wanted was him.

She valued her skills and would love to keep the job, but what was one short-term job compared to a lifetime of happiness with the man she loved. She closed her eyes and enjoyed the thrill that shot through her. She loved him.

He was her friend. Her confident. Her biggest supporter. Most of all, he was the perfect lover, and he made her want to do everything right. Including coming clean to everyone in their lives, because it was the right thing to do.

"Honey?"

She turned around, but stayed by the window. "Morning."

He rose up on his elbows. His mouth softened and his eyes heated. She cupped her elbows in her hands. She'd never get used to that look. If someone asked her what love looked like, she'd describe the way he gazed at her. As if she couldn't do anything wrong.

"You're beautiful," he said.

She smiled and walked to the bed, sitting on the edge and smoothing the hair off his forehead. "You make me feel beautiful."

He pulled her down beside him, cradling her in his arm. She laid her head on his chest. Warm from sleep, he comforted her in a way nothing else did.

"What were you thinking?" he asked.

She wasn't ready to discuss her decision, so she shared the other thing that had kept her up half the night. "What my mom went through was horrible."

"Yeah, it was," he whispered.

She traced the shape of a heart on his chest, over his left pectoral muscle. "It wasn't my fault she died," she whispered back.

He stiffened and pushed her shoulders up, so she'd look at him. "Have you believed differently this whole time?"

She nodded.

"Aw, honey." He pulled her back tight to his chest. "I had no idea…"

"I never told anyone. Not even Drew." She rubbed her cheek against him, snuggling closer. "I know she had cancer. The doctors were blunt on what would happen, the different stages we could expect. Even Mom prepared me for her leaving us. I can't even say I was surprised to wake up that night and find her already gone. But when I tried to breathe life into her, and I was pushing on her chest, praying with everything I had that I could bring her back just long enough to tell her I loved her…that girl, that daughter, that sister, believed I'd failed everyone."

He kissed the top of her head. "It was her time, unfortunately. There was nothing you could've done. She was ready to go and be at peace, and tired from the strain of fighting the cancer."

"I know. I think I've finally accepted that it was selfish to keep her any longer. I'd never want her to suffer," she said. "I have you to thank for that."

"Me?"

She moistened her lips. "I asked my mom one time what love felt like, and she told me it was every emotion a human could experience at extreme levels. You laugh louder, you cry harder, you get angry easier, and you love deeper. Until you've experienced them all on the same person, it would never be true love."

"I like that." He smoothed the hair off her cheek.

"So, I've come to the conclusion, Mr. Big Guy Satchel, that I love you." She moved up and kissed him on the lips. "You've given it all to me and more."

"I love you too. Always have and will forever." He kissed her harder.

He stroked her back. She saw the questions in his eyes. The ones she wasn't ready to answer or hear. He controlled everything they did, but the decision she had to make would come from her without anyone's help. Her mom would be proud of her, because what she didn't tell Gary was the best advice of all.

Her mom told her when she found the man that would wrap her heart in the safety of his hands, she should do anything in her power never to lose that gift. She didn't plan on losing Gary. Ever.

She kissed him again, and he responded. She closed her eyes and lost herself in the heat that flooded her body.

His hands worked their way up under the shirt of Gary's that she wore and she went willingly, her body shaping to his. Each stroke of his tongue gave way to her pulse racing.

Wanting began in her head, moved to her chest, and settled low in her belly and spiraled out in all directions. Her breasts, tender to the touch, ached. Her sex throbbed in the telling combination of tension and dampness.

He cupped her rear, bringing her on top of him. His fingers were warm against her bare skin, moving deliberately across her ribs, then taking the weight of her breasts. Everything about his attention to her body was exactly what she craved. His thumbs brushed her sensitive nipples. She arched her back and moaned.

He raised up on his elbows, taking her right nipple in his mouth. He drew waves of pleasure from deep inside of her. The rush of heat and wetness between her legs increased and she reached between them to enclose his length in her hand.

She had to hold on, because they were both moving. Her rocking. Him taking more of her breast in his mouth. She found it difficult to breathe.

Gary rolled her over onto her back, him on top of her, face to face. He lowered himself so he could kiss her breasts again. Then he put his hand on her belly. Her legs relaxed, opening herself up to his fingers.

He slipped between the folds of skin and found her swollen center.

God, he was good with his hands.

He circled, teased, around and around, moving lightly but determined. Barely skimming the exact spot she needed. She raised her hands and grabbed the headboard, shuddering as his touch came faster, harder, more precise.

He shifted, taking her mouth with his. The sweep of his tongue, the roughness of his unshaven jaw, and the intensity of his concentration won out and her self-control left.

She opened her legs wider and arched her hips. Her orgasm hovered out of reach.

He read her mind, and only left her long enough to snag a condom off the nightstand, apply the protection, and return to her. Then he was in her, filling her, taking her deeper than he'd ever been. She hung on to his arms planted on each side of her head.

Tension built and she orgasmed a second before he did. Both of them locked in each other's arms, her pleasure squeezing him, making him shudder. If she thought loving Gary was the best feeling in the world, she was wrong. Having Gary inside of her, loving her, giving her everything, was the best freaking gift he could give her.

Chapter Twenty-One

Fourth down, thirty seconds on the clock in the final quarter, Gary leaned down, put his fist to the turf, and his gaze on the middle of the player in front of him. His arm shook and he widened his feet, taking more of his weight on his legs. The doctor had okay'd him for play, but already his arm showed weakness from playing today.

Thankfully, he had four days before the next game. He'd take it easy in practice and ice it good. Maybe have Angie work her magic on his shoulder.

The whistle blew. He tagged the offensive lineman, pivoted on his heel, and dove on the next player. He grunted, landing on his side.

The referee's whistle blew. He pushed off the player and turned around. Time out was called. He jogged over to the huddle.

"Satchel and Connor, heavy on the D, bulldoze through. Porter, swing toward the right, you're going to switch with Satchel. Nail their ass, and we'll beat the clock. Do not let their QB throw the fucking ball. They get over the line and we'll be in OT. I got a blonde waiting for me after the game, and I do not want to wait." George Pierce stepped back, breaking the group.

Gary nodded and jogged back to the line, glancing at the scoreboard. Five seconds.

He'd have to be fast.

He slipped in his mouth guard. Adrenaline spiked, and he bounced on the toes of his shoes before bending over to assume the position. He rocked back and forth, ready to pounce.

The other team's quarterback called out the play. A gut instinct had him shifting his weight to his left side. He ignored the tremor in his arm.

The ball went live. He hit the other player lower, throwing him to the left, making room through the line. Connor went down hard in front of him. He leaped over the tangled bodies, stretching, and snagged the quarterback. As he rolled, he turned, searching for the ball.

Through the players, he couldn't see anything. Not the ball, not the receivers, nothing.

The Cowboys' quarterback cussed as the blare of the air horn over the speaker got the crowd cheering. Gary pushed to his feet and quickly got caught in the mob of players.

"Right on, man." Conner slapped the top of Gary's helmet. "Two point lead, and we're right in the top of the ladder."

He grinned, taking the slaps, the pats, the helmet bumps. In the crowd, he walked in the direction he got shoved. There was no pain in his body, his energy was restored, and he was flying high off the win.

Acceptance came freely, but it was the fulfillment of providing a need for someone else that filled him. Ever since he was young, knowing that he accomplished what others expected drove him to be better, until all he could do was rely on the fact that he could make things happen for other people to find his worth in the world. Whether that was winning the Super Bowl, mentoring children to strive in school, or putting a smile on Angie's face. When he could affect others, he belonged. That feeling, that need, had been lacking growing up where nothing he did pleased anyone.

"Good game, Satchel." Coach slapped his ass on his way past him.

He unsnapped his helmet and peeled it off his head. "Thanks, Coach."

As he always did while playing a home game, he headed to the wall. A young boy held a pen and paper over the railing. He stretched up and took the offer from the kid.

"Enjoy the game?" He scribbled his name on the paper and handed it back.

The kid bobbed his head. "Thanks."

"You're welcome." He high fived the teenager beside the boy and moved down the line.

One after the other, he signed his autograph for every person who had a scrap of paper. He asked a question in return, smiled at the answers, and then moved to the next person waiting to get their moment with him. He stopped in front of a voluptuous woman with her brown hair braided over her shoulder and decked out in Seahawk gear.

"Thanks for coming," he said.

She leaned over, pulled her sweatshirt down, and displayed her cleavage. "Can you sign?"

He chuckled, shaking his head in amusement. "Pen?"

The gentleman beside her handed him a pen. He grabbed the bottom rail and propped the toe of his shoe against the wall, heaving himself higher. With great care, he signed 'Gary' on one breast and 'Satchel' on the other.

Before he could jump down, she kissed his cheek. He landed on the ground, smiling. Women were crazy. Always there wanting his attention and doing whatever they could to try and get noticed. He'd taken them home, he'd slept with them in his car before heading back to the condo, and played out their fantasy of having sex with a professional football player. Though he never remembered their names. Hell, half the time, he couldn't tell you what color hair they'd had.

They used each other for their own needs, and he went home alone. Before Angie, he'd stayed away from relationships. While he'd entertained himself when he knew Angie was out of his reach, he'd still believed no one else would do for him. He was right. Only one woman captured his heart.

He waved to the crowd and made his way to the tunnel to hit the shower. Once he entered the walkway under the stadium, he slowed down and enjoyed the afterglow of the win. The other guys were already unsuiting, and in the locker room. They never stayed after a game to wave or chat with the fans, preferring to have their own party away from the stadium. Sometimes he joined them, most times he wanted to share the night with someone and ended up either alone or unfulfilled.

Now he had Angie to go home with, and she was the only person he wanted to share his win with tonight.

"Do you think if I pulled down my shirt, you'd sign my chest?" Angie's voice floated toward him.

He raised his gaze and found her leaning against the wall beside the door to the locker room. He glanced around, making sure they were alone. "I'd sign anything you want to show me."

She remained leaning against the brick and tilted her head. "What if I asked you to kiss me?"

"I never kissed her. She kissed me." His fingers tightened around the guard on his helmet, wishing he'd jumped a little sooner and skipped the kiss from the other woman and saved Angie the worry. "They're fans. That's all."

Angie's mouth softened. "I know."

She brushed a lock of her hair out of her face. Exhaustion from the game came with the contentment of knowing she understood what kind of man he was. He'd no sooner mess around on her than cut out his own heart.

I love you, he mouthed.

She held up her hand, and crooked her finger to him. "I know that too."

He took the five steps separating them, until he stood in front of her. "I also love playing football."

"I'm not asking you to give it up or to stop being a decent guy to your fans." She laid her hand flat on his stomach, below his pads. "Just reminding you that you have me."

"Don't need reminders, because no matter what, I'm not letting you go." He dropped his helmet and cupped her face with both his hands. "We'll figure something out. It's our time."

Her brows arched. He smoothed the line at the corner of her eye with his finger. He'd never get enough of her.

"I should be telling you what a good game you played, and how I loved watching you." Her neck muscles constricted and she gave him an extra-long blink. "But I was stuck in the locker room rubbing down Jeff Lowry's leg."

He growled, pulling her forward until he had her pressed against the front of him. "Don't really want to hear about what you and Lowry did."

"You know what I mean," she mumbled into the front of his jersey.

"Yeah." He stroked her back, enjoying the feel of her relaxing against him.

They were out in the open. Anyone could walk around the corner and spot them together. He ran through a list of excuses on why he'd be hugging the team's massage therapist, but no one would believe him. One look at Angie, and they'd know exactly where his thoughts headed.

"Uh, baby?" Angie sighed and turned her head, although she never left his embrace.

He grunted in reply, while kissing the top of her head.

"You do know you stink, right?" She pulled her head back and grinned. "Why don't you hit the shower? I need to go back in and check on Lowry. He's soaking in ice."

He kissed her quickly. "Later, honey."

"Later." She picked up his helmet and handed it to him. "You go first. I'll wait a few minutes and go in after you."

Walking away from her was the hardest thing he'd had to do today. He tackled people on reflex. He competed because something inside of him drove him to be the best he could be.

He followed the rules, because that's how you play fair. To hide his relationship with Angie from his teammates, the coaches, the owner, went against the kind of person he wanted to be, and he hated it.

He swung through the door to chaos and good spirits. Morgan snapped him with a towel, and he lifted his chin, dodging the stinging snap. At his locker, he punched Pierce in the arm to get his attention and turned around expectantly. Unsuiting was a routine they all went through with help. The quarterback pulled Gary's jersey over his head.

"Thanks." Gary set out to remove his shoulder pads. "Good game."

"You too, man. Saved our win...again." Pierce clicked his tongue. "The girls are going wild out there. Better shower up and go get you one."

He chuckled. "Yeah."

He stripped down and walked to the showers naked. There was only one girl he wanted, and she hadn't even seen him during his big moment.

Chapter Twenty-Two

Worried that she couldn't give Gary the attention he deserved to celebrate the winning game, Angie hurried through treating Lowry for his strained hamstring and had the security guard walk her out to the parking lot. She slowed down at her car and rummaged through her bag.

"Thanks again for walking me out." She held up her key.

Stewart, a couple years younger than Angie, ducked his chin. "See you next game."

She smiled and turned around. After unlocking her door, she glanced behind her. Stewart jogged back to the stadium.

She dove into the car, found a piece of paper and pen, and wrote a message. Then she studied the area. One player hung out at the exit, but a woman kept him distracted by fawning all over him. The others in the parking lot were either pulling their cars out, or packing their things in the trunk of their cars. She hurried over to Gary's car, slipped the paper under the windshield wiper, and ran back to her car.

She dove inside and smiled to herself. It was a stupid idea to leave him a message. He'd be home in less than a half hour. They'd have all the privacy they needed inside his condominium. Except, she wanted to do more for him. He deserved a woman who could support him fully and stroke his ego after one of his best preseason games ever.

At least, she'd heard the talk about how he played. She'd tried to catch a glimpse of him after halftime, but first Sampson and then Lowry came to her with injuries. It was to be expected. Start of the season injuries were always high. Their bodies took a lot of abuse after having a couple months off to rest.

Gary's body was no exception. She got to see what he went through on a daily basis. He tried to hide a lot of his aches, but she'd noticed. The groan after pushing himself out of bed. The grimace when he grabbed her to roll her over on the couch. But none of his discomfort stopped him from showering attention on her.

She started the car, and drove toward the gate. Three other cars were ahead of her. She gazed in her rearview mirror, and seeing the area clear, made a U-turn. Her heart raced. There were rules that they had two hours to leave the grounds. They were usually out of there within an hour. That gave her some time before the gate shut, but she wanted no one to know where she was going. It was too easy for someone to catch her and she didn't want to end her career this way. She wanted to stay classy and professional. A rendezvous with a player, no matter their relationship, wouldn't be viewed as being responsible.

She drove around to section B. The gate attendee had already left, since they only kept one gate open for the team. She parked in the shadow of the stadium and shut off the car's engine. In the silence, her breath came fast and heavy. She'd never done something like this.

Sure, she'd broken a few rules, went swimming at hotels she wasn't staying at or begged her way backstage at a concert. She chalked those times up to teenage fun. Now she was an adult, had a job with the Seahawks, and she was hiding from everyone.

She tapped her fingers against the steering wheel. What if Gary didn't notice the note she left him or someone else found it before he did?

She reached for her keys, but stopped herself from turning the car back on. No, he'd come. He'd already finished dressing when she had left the locker room.

Several minutes passed, and finally she saw headlights sweep the parking lot in front of her and his car appeared around the corner. She smiled, reaching for the door handle. Excitement and nerves had her stomach flipping.

She shut her door quietly when Gary pulled up beside her. She walked over. He rolled the window down, concern etched in his gaze.

"What's wrong?" he asked.

She leaned through the window and kissed him. His hand came up and tangled in her hair. She softened her lips, sucking on his bottom lip. The thrill of doing something out here, away from the others, but close enough to share Gary with the sport he loved shot through her. He deserved what others offered him freely, and she wanted to be the one to give it to him.

She reached down and ran her hand over the crotch of his jeans. Her lips curved over his as he hardened from her touch. If she'd had any doubts that he wouldn't be up for her surprise, they fled.

Unable to unbutton his jeans with one hand, she pulled away, opened the door so she was closer to him, and gazed at him. His eyes softened. "Your note didn't say anything about this."

"Surprise," she whispered, working his buttons loose. "A man who wins the game and puts his team at higher odds going into the season deserves more than me saying, 'good game,' don't you think?"

He chuckled, lifting his hips and tugging his jeans down a smidge. She watched his gaze intensify as she leaned over farther, opening her mouth.

His fingers tightened in her hair. "Jesus, honey…"

She took his cock in her mouth. He bucked off the seat and quickly came down, his whole body relaxing with each caress of her lips. She sprawled her hands on his thighs, keeping him in place. The power in his legs made her own tremble, and she placed her knee on the edge of the doorframe of the car.

"Honey…" He smoothed the hair back from her face. "Damn, that feels good."

She sucked harder, taking her time, enjoying the moment as much as Gary. Even though he'd never tell her she owed him, she hadn't forgotten about their sexy time in the locker room when he'd ignored his own needs and pleasured her.

She tilted her head, taking more of him on each down stroke. His muscles quivered under her hands, until he pulled her off him.

She jerked her gaze to him. "But—"

He laid his finger over her lips, and backed her out of the car, climbing out himself. He took her shoulders and turned her around until her back was facing him. She gazed at him over her shoulder as he placed her hands on the side of her car.

"What are you doing?" she asked.

His hands went around her waist to her jeans. She shivered when she realized what he planned to do.

Her breath came fast. "Someone will catch us."

He pulled her pants down to her knees, taking her panties with them. "No one's back here. The cars block us from both sides."

Okay, she really loved this idea.

He put his foot between her legs, pushing her left foot out to widen her stance. She dropped her head between her outstretched arms and arched her back at the sound of a condom wrapper ripping. She smiled. "Are you always prepared?"

"With you around…yeah." He caressed her from bare waist to hip. Her arms quivered and her lower body vibrated. Out here in the open, risking everything for this one moment was the hottest thing she'd ever done.

His hard heat slid along her wetness. She leaned forward, and gasped when he slid inside of her. He stilled, and she closed her eyes thinking the best feeling in the world was when he was inside of her and they were connected.

Slowly, barely moving at first, he thrust and withdrew. The roughness of his jeans skimmed the back of her thighs with each movement. Her breasts strained against her bra, sensitive and throbbing. She pushed back against him, and heard his swift intake of breath. Her lower stomach pulsated and she reached for the pleasure he was giving her. Then his arm wrapped around her, and his hand went between her legs. He plunged inside of her, withdrawing until he almost left her, and then gave her every single inch of him.

Her hands slid against the smooth surface of her car. She rose on her toes as he moved within her. His finger was doing crazy, wicked things to her, driving her wild. He was everywhere, touching her, holding her, taking her with him. Heat grew inside her core, and her muscles tightened. Clenched around him, she peaked and lost her breath right before her whole world exploded into tiny delicious bolts of pleasure starting deep inside of her and flowing to her limbs.

She sagged at the same time he held her hips and thrust into her, holding her to him. His body shuddered behind her and it was the most wonderful experience of her life. A carefree giggle grew and she let it out.

Gary wrapped his arms around her and chuckled above her. They were both shaking from exhaustion, barely holding themselves up. If he let go of her, she'd crumble at his feet.

"I lost my jeans around my ankles," he said.

She dipped her chin and glanced down. "It's okay, your ass is white compared to the rest of you—if anyone saw it they'd swear it was the moon."

"Smart ass." He laughed, pulling out of her without letting her go. "Shit. I'm weak. My legs are trembling."

"Ha. You have an excuse. You played in a game. I stood in the locker room." She took a step away, leaned over, and pulled her jeans up.

Gary went to his car, got rid of the condom, and came back to her. Before she could say anything, he kissed her hard.

She murmured her pleasure against his lips, and smiled when he pulled away. "That was crazy."

"Yeah." He laughed, running his hand through his hair. "I dreamed about having you here, after a game, all to myself."

She walked to him and slipped her arms around him. "What did I do in your dream?"

"Well…" He sighed. "First you blew me in the car—"

"You didn't let me finish that," she said.

"Right." He cleared his throat. "Then I took you against the car."

She smiled. "We did that."

"Yeah." He chuckled. "After we finished, I put you on the hood of the car and had you again. There might've been—" he jerked his head toward the stadium "—a fourth act out on the fifty yard line."

"All in one night? Four times?" She leaned back and gazed at him. His mouth twitched, hiding his confession, and she laughed. "After a game?"

He looked away smiling into the night. "I said they were dreams."

She pulled him down and kissed him. "I'll make sure I add more protein in your oatmeal, big guy, and I'll see if I can fulfill all your dreams."

He kissed her one more time, slapped her ass, and lifted his chin toward her car. "Let's go home. I'll follow."

She walked away, looking over her shoulder at him. "Promise?"

He slid into the driver's seat of his own vehicle and flashed his killer smile. "Promise."

She laid her hand over her heart and got into her car. Past the gate, she entered the freeway and removed her hand from her chest. The smile on her face, however, she wore all the way back to Gary's condominium.

Chapter Twenty-Three

Four days later, Angie walked down the corridor to the locker room with Gary. She pressed her lips together instead of commenting on how loose and unencumbered Gary moved now that the swelling in his shoulder had gone down and he'd stayed away from any contact during practice the last two days. As far as the other guys knew, she hadn't seen him since yesterday at practice and was taking the time to see how he was doing.

Morgan and Pierce led the way, and Lowry followed behind them. She carried her bag and kept her gaze straight ahead of her. After tonight's game, the NFL season started for real. Every game counted.

"Hey, Angie," Jeff Lowry said behind her.

She stopped and turned around. Gary hesitated, seemed to want to stay, and then reluctantly continued walking to the door. She pushed away the awkward position and smiled. "How's the leg, Jeff?"

"Better. I'm going in and having the doc look at it in hopes I can put some time on the field before we play the Raiders next." Jeff went quiet and glanced behind him. "I was wondering…I mean, I know you can't date any of the players, but maybe we could have dinner or a drink sometime? As a thank you for all your help getting me back in shape to play, I mean."

She inhaled swiftly. "I'm sorry, Jeff. Since this job is new to me, I don't want to jeopardize my place with the team. I need the job, and although we can be friends, I don't want anyone to mistake us going out as something more."

"Hey, it's okay." Jeff shrugged and grinned. "I'm not the only guy on the team talking about asking you out. I just thought I'd beat the other guys."

She shook her head. "I'm not a game for the guys to see if they can win."

"Hell, we know that." He squeezed her arm. "Maybe after the season's over, huh?"

She leaned closer and nudged him with her arm. "Go see the doctor, and warm up your leg."

Jeff walked off and she watched him until he disappeared behind the locker room door. She sagged against the wall. She was a liar. Nobody was going to understand if she and Gary ever found a way to go public. If she had extra time, she'd hunt for a new job—even though she loved working for the Seahawks. Because more than she needed the money from working, she needed to tell the world she was in love.

If she had to, she'd go back to Deadhorse and live there forever if it meant Gary was with her. She closed her eyes a beat and thumped the back of her head against the wall. How stupid was she to think being back in Seattle, where her friends and faster pace of life were, would bring her happiness. A month ago, she'd had no idea what she was really looking for was love.

She had no desire to go out without Gary, and Jules no longer had time for her, because she was too busy scoping out men at clubs, which Angie did not want to do. Her scope was solidly fixated on the man she loved.

Besides, Gary's career came first. He had more to lose than she did if she decided to put an end to their private relationship. Yet, there was one way she could fix all their problems. She could quietly quit her job, and nothing would happen to him.

"Angie?" a masculine voice said.

She opened her eyes, blinked, and pushed away from the wall. "Grayson?"

Grayson Schyler, Wimbledon tennis champion and one of Gary's best friends, stood in front of her in jeans and a leather jacket, his sunstreaked blond hair pushed off his forehead and an adorable baby riding atop his shoulders.

"Are you here to watch Gary too?" Grayson looked past her. "Is your brother here?"

She shook her head. "No, it's just me. I'm the new massage therapist for the Seahawks."

"No kidding?" He grinned, flashing a perfect white smile that put her at ease. "Shauna and I flew up to surprise Gary."

"That's great." She smiled at the baby and stood on tiptoe to tickle his adorable chubby cheek. "Whose baby?"

"This is Trevor, my son." Grayson swept Trevor down and held him on his arm. "Can you wave, Trev?"

Trevor stuck his fingers in his mouth and drooled. Her heart melted and she looked up at Grayson. "I had no idea. Last time I saw you it was almost two years ago—you weren't even married or anything."

"Shauna swept back into my life. I had no choice but to marry her." Grayson winked, looking like a man who was deeply in love.

Angie tilted her head. "Wait. Shauna…the girl all the guys kid you about? Your stalker?"

"The very one." Grayson chuckled. "You'll have to meet my wife. She's up in the stands, along with Juan and Dana." Gary bounced Trevor who'd begun to whine. "I'm walking Trevor around to keep him quiet. He's teething."

"This is so wild." She pressed her hand to her forehead. "Juan's married too? Why haven't I heard any of this?"

"From what I hear, you were living in Seattle the last few years." Grayson laughed softly. "Gary's kept us updated, plus Drew came to our wedding and mentioned you were now a massage therapist at some swanky place downtown. Everything is changing. We're all settling down…except Bruce and Crista. Dominic's not here tonight, but he got hitched and lives in Cottage Grove now. Shauna's best friends with his wife, Diana."

"That's…crazy," she said.

The locker door banged open. Gary stormed out. His gaze connected on her, took in Grayson, and acknowledged his arrival with a chin lift, and he strode her way. She squeezed Grayson's hand. "Excuse me for a moment."

She met Gary a few feet away. "What's wrong?"

"We were caught on a security tape the other night. Apparently, they wanted to watch us for a few days to see how we acted together while I practiced before confronting me." His mouth hardened. "I knew this would happen."

"Oh my God." She covered her mouth.

"I'm sure they'll be talking to you next. I've already told them it was nothing. Just me getting caught up in the win, and taking advantage of you," he whispered. "They understand the adrenaline, and will be much more lenient with me."

She dropped her hand. "What?"

"If you tell them we've had no relations until that night, and now it's over and done, they might keep you on. Maybe put you on probation if you stay away from me," he said.

"I can't do that," she blurted.

She looked at Grayson standing there and groaned. Nothing like spilling their secret to another person, and having one more thing to worry about.

Gary nodded at Grayson. "He's not going to say anything."

"I know that, but—"

"It's over, honey. You'll go in there and if they ask, it was a one night fling after the game and meant nothing to you." Gary straightened. "I need to get back in there before they notice I'm missing. I'll talk to you at home, and get you set up at a hotel until you can figure out where you want to live."

She stared after him with her mouth open, not believing what was happening. There was always a risk. She'd gone into the relationship knowing this day could happen. Her idea to surprise him after the game had backfired. She dashed away the tear that fell down her cheek. Their relationship—whether secret or public—was over.

Instead of feeling relief that she no longer had to hide how much she loved Gary, she ached inside. Why did it feel like Gary had just walked out of her life, for good?

"Angie?" Grayson put his hand on her arm. "I take it you two are together."

She nodded, unable to speak.

"Can I do anything?" he asked.

She shook her head and pasted on a smile she in no way felt and then lied again. "It'll be okay."

But the way Gary made the situation sound was awful. She wasn't a fling. She wasn't his fangirl. He'd cut her off, and wanted to discontinue their relationship. He wanted to put her up in a hotel. He wanted her gone. He wanted her to lie about their love.

"I need to go in," she said, her voice cracking.

"Okay." Grayson rubbed her back. "Tell Gary I'll…I'll call him tomorrow. We're all staying at the Hyatt."

She nodded and walked away. Numb and confused, she had no idea what was going to happen now. Gary had been upset, and she'd put his career in jeopardy. If she were smart, she'd walk in there and tell the truth and end the gossip.

She loved Gary.

She opened the door and stepped into the locker room. The muggy heat and putrid odors swept over her. She'd need this job if Gary was no longer going to see her.

Seeing him every day and not having him in her life would kill her. She motioned Lowry over to the bench, but before she could join him, John and Gary's coach ordered her into the office. She walked across the locker room with a thousand pounds resting on her shoulders. The only thing she could do was go along with Gary's story, and hope they understood it was a moment's bad decision. If she survived from a broken heart that long, she could figure out what to do next.

Chapter Twenty-Four

Gary walked out of the elevator at the Hyatt hotel onto the third floor, carrying Angie's two bags of luggage she'd thrown together in a fit of anger after he'd informed her it was over and they had to go their separate ways to make sure she kept her job. He clamped his teeth together to keep from saying what was really on his mind—that he hated sending her away, and he wanted her with him, where she belonged.

John had put Angie on notice. Coach had told him to get rid of the girl. The situation was out of his hands, and the only thing he could do was distance himself. If he continued to live with Angie, there was no way he'd fix their problem. Moving her to the hotel was for the best.

Angie stopped outside room 348 and swiped her key card through the lock. He took one step inside and placed her bags on the floor. His chest tightened and he gave the room one sweep to make sure everything was okay for her stay and she'd be comfortable.

"Remember to call room service and order something to eat. I've already paid your bill, so don't go without." He took in her red-rimmed eyes, knowing she hadn't cried in front of him and it hurt to know she was suffering.

She turned around and crossed her arms. "I'm fine. You can leave."

He shoved his hands deep in his front pockets. There were a lot of things he could do, but leaving was right up there with getting an elbow in his diaphragm and getting taken out of the game. "It's the right thing for us to do, honey."

She lifted her chin and refused to comment. He inhaled deeply and looked away from the pain etched in her eyes. He'd always known it would come to this. If it wasn't her job, it was his risk of getting involved with his best friend's little sister and tearing them all apart. Drew was coming around to supporting them both, but if he screwed up and Angie lost her job, it was another thing he'd have to own up to with Drew. No matter what happened, someone was going to get hurt.

"You'll be okay?" he asked.

She shook her head. "No."

"Angie, I—"

"Don't." She held her hand up, stopping him from saying any more. "I've already told you that I think we're making a big mistake. I can quit. I'd rather leave my job under my own power than stop what we have together."

"You can't. This job means everything to you, and once you have time to figure that out, you'll realize that we need to stop seeing each other. Remember how you felt when you lived in Deadhorse with Drew?"

She looked away. He stepped forward. It was unnatural to stay away from her. Before they got together, he would've comforted her. After they got together, he would've comforted her. Now, he had no right to comfort her, and the hole in his heart threatened to cave in.

"I love you," he whispered. "But I don't want you to…"

"What?" she asked.

He shook his head. "There are things in my life I regret. Time I wasted being angry and defiant to everyone in my life, because I thought I deserved better. I don't want you to go through the same thing, and I'm afraid a year or two from now, you'll look back and wish you'd made other choices."

"I won't." Her lips quivered. "I'll never regret you or the time we had. But you leaving me like this, I'll never forget it. Every time I go to bed alone, I'll know that you're not with me. Every time I wake up in the middle of the night and realize your arms aren't around me, I'll know I'm truly alone. I've been there before, and I hated it."

"Honey, you've accepted why you have nightmares and realized your mom dying wasn't your fault. You've slept well for the last couple of weeks," he said.

"Tell my heart that we didn't just die. That I didn't lose you then." She rubbed her palm down her cheek. "I love you."

"I know." That knowledge killed him. He backed away and put his hand on the door handle. "Make sure you lock up."

Then he hurried out of the room before he did something he'd regret. Halfway down the hallway, his phone rang. He grabbed and pushed the button before he could stop himself.

"Angie?" he said.

"No, it's Grayson," the deep voice said.

He stopped outside the elevator. "Hey, sorry about not calling. I had some stuff to do after the game."

"I heard, man." Grayson sighed. "You doing okay?"

"Yeah." He blew out his breath. "Short story, Angie and I were secretly seeing each other…hell, she was living with me, and with her new job, she's not allowed to date any of the players. Someone saw a tape of us messing around after the game, and she could lose her contract with the Seahawks."

"That's what I figured with what Angie told me. Sorry to hear about it though, Satchel. Is there no way around it?" Grayson asked.

"I walked away from her so she can keep her job," he said. "It's killing me."

"Shit." Grayson paused. "Are you serious about her?"

Was he serious? He gazed up at the ceiling. She was his everything. He couldn't imagine life without her, and even if he weren't sleeping with her, he'd find any way to stay in contact. That'd never change. She'd started out as a friend and now that he'd had her, they'd grown closer and he'd confessed his feelings, he wasn't willing to let that go. *But I did.*

"I love her," he said quietly. "I've loved her my entire life, but only recently been able to show her what she means to me. Hell, I thought I'd died when she returned my feelings."

Grayson cussed. "You need to talk?"

"No." He rubbed the back of his neck. "I'm going to go home and crash, try to figure everything out, so I have some answers for her tomorrow. She doesn't understand why I'm pulling back from her. It's all or nothing with her."

"Well, if you need anything, we're at the Hyatt until tomorrow night. Juan and Dana are here too. We wanted to catch your game tonight, and then we promised the girls they could spend a day shopping tomorrow. We'll get together next time we come up, okay?"

He looked down the hallway. "I'm standing in the Hyatt right now. Third floor by the elevator."

"Hang on," Grayson said.

A few seconds later a door opened at the end of the hallway. Gary disconnected the call and walked to meet Grayson who appeared in the corridor. They clasped hands in front of room 348.

"Good to see you, but I wish it was a happier time for you." Grayson shook his head. "I'd buy you a beer, but I don't think that's a good idea tonight."

"Yeah. Probably not." Gary hitched his chin toward the door. "Angie's in there. I'm not really wanting to walk away, you know."

Grayson nodded. "Want me to send Shauna and Dana over to talk with her?"

He cringed. The last thing he wanted was more women telling Angie how much he'd screwed up. Yet, Angie needed the support. He put his hand on the door. "She could use some friends right now. She's hurting."

Grayson slapped his arm. "Done. Go home. Get some rest. Deal with this shit tomorrow."

"Yeah." He moved away from the door. "Thanks, man."

Gary skipped taking the elevator down to the lobby, and instead pushed through the door at the end of the hall and took the stairs. His legs weak from playing tonight, he took his time. That was his excuse anyway. The real reason he hesitated on leaving the hotel was because he wanted to go back up to room 348 and be with Angie.

He kept making his descent down the steps. She'd never understand about the bitterness that piled up on your shoulders until it seemed even the simplest things were a burden. He'd grown up regretting being born to a mom who had too many problems to worry about her own child. Then later, the bitterness of being part of the system, shoved into a house that only provided the basics—food, clothes, roof over his head.

It was too much to ask her to get rid of everything she loved to settle for him. He was a professional athlete, on the road more times than he was home during the season, always giving his energy to a sport that took everything from him. He still wasn't sure he could provide the right amount of love, or provide her with a family, when he had nothing in his past that showed he was capable of giving another person everything they needed.

He could play football.

He could win.

He could bust his ass every day to make other people's life happier.

He pushed out into the cool night. His knees wobbled, and he forced himself to keep walking away. This time he wasn't sure he'd survive, because he'd left his heart up in room 348.

Chapter Twenty-Five

The dim lamp in the sitting room of the hotel room barely cast any light on Angie's visit with Shauna and Dana. She sank farther into the corner of the couch. Talk about awkward.

She'd talked to Grayson and Juan's wives for the last two hours, and she'd never met them before in her life. Their husbands? Sure, about twice a year, she'd hang out with them when Drew and Gary had them visit Seattle, but they weren't her friends. They were Gary's.

These two women were strangers, and yet she found herself leaning on them for support because she had no one else at the moment to care about her messed up life.

"You have to be firm. Lay it all on the line." Dana, her blonde hair hanging straight down her back, paced in front of the coffee table. "I know Gary. He's famous, but he's a boy. A boy in a big body. That means he's not going to explain himself, and he thinks you can read his mind."

Shauna, dressed in a sexy yoga outfit, nodded, cuddling a sleeping Trevor to her chest. Her eyes were tired, but determined. "Grayson's just as stubborn. It took me years to convince him he loved me. Trust me, you want to grab Gary by the balls and tell him how it's going to be right now, or every day he'll get stronger and more determined about his screwed up theory that you don't belong together."

Angie rubbed her hands over her face. "I'm going to quit the job. Gary is more important than money or my time. I've known this since I was younger, even before I slept with him. He's kept me sane, out of trouble, and supported me in everything I've done. He even got me the damn job, and look what it's doing to us."

"Wait." Dana stopped walking and pointed at her. "Nobody said anything to you about your—" she twirled her finger in the air "—hot sex at the stadium, right?"

She shook her head. "No. Gary was the only one who they talked to, and they warned him if he continued seeing me, they'd get rid of me. I broke my contract. They'll forgive him, he's their star, but I'm replaceable."

Gary talked about her regrets if they stayed together and she got fired, but the only thing she wanted to take back was her dumb idea to risk everything for a blow job and incredible, wicked sex against the side of the car. Why she'd thought that was a good idea was beyond thinking about. She had to be smarter; more mature. She was dating a professional football player, not a teenager. She groaned. "I can't even think."

Shauna stood up slowly, covering Trevor with a blanket. "I need to put this little guy down for the night and hope he sleeps for a few hours."

Angie stood. "I'm going to go to bed too."

"Sleep. That will help you think better." Dana approached her and wrapped her arms around her shoulders, drawing her close. "If you need us, we'll skip shopping tomorrow. Just call us. I put my number in your phone earlier."

She nodded against Dana's shoulder. Her eyes misted over again and she gave her new friend a squeeze. "Thank you. Both of you."

Shauna kissed her cheek. "We've got your back. If anyone knows what it's like to keep an egotistical man in line, it's us."

Angie forced a smile, walked them to the door, said goodnight, and latched the door. Gary wasn't egotistical. He was the kindest, gentlest man she knew. He'd always been that way. Sometimes she wondered if his size pushed him to take things slower for fear his temper would get the best of him and he'd hurt someone. Yet, she'd never seen him even argue with someone. It was like he saved all his energy for the field and for the opposing team.

Grabbing her phone off the table, she walked to the bedroom. She looked at the time. Two-thirty in the morning,

She was going to be dead to the world tomorrow if she didn't get any sleep. Her stomach quivered and she pressed her hand to her belly. How was she going to sleep without Gary?

With the first game of the NFL season the day after tomorrow, she needed to get her life straightened out. She flopped down on the bed. There was no use undressing and crawling under the covers. She doubted if she could sleep. Even if she managed to doze off, she'd probably wake up in a worse mood than she was already in.

She turned her classic rock playlist on low and scrolled through her messages on her phone. Everyone she knew had texted her the last couple of days. Her dad, Drew, Jules, Jeff Lowry...she clicked on his name.

Heard a rumor about U. True?

She deleted the message, wondering how he'd gotten her phone number. She groaned. *Shit.*

She'd given every player on the team who'd needed a massage a way to contact her in case they wanted to set up a time to have her work on them when it was a day off from practice and games. The overtime wasn't required of her, but she knew how important playing was to each one of them. It was imperative that the Seahawks go the distance.

Her phone vibrated and she shut off the music and sat up. She stared at the screen, holding her breath as she read the incoming text from Gary.

Won't call. Just want to tell U...goodnight.

Her hand shook. She exhaled and quickly tapped on the keys. *Wait!*

Several seconds passed, and she was afraid he wouldn't respond when she read, *What?*

What was she going to say? She missed him? She was sorry? She wanted to go back to his condominium to sleep with him?

She worked her lips in worry and typed. *I'll make things right. Promise.*

Before she could lie down, he replied. *Not you. Me. Don't say anything to them. I'll Fix it.*

How typical of him. He took the blame on himself, and wanted to sort her life out. She wasn't incapable of taking care of herself. Sure, he'd gotten the job for her—she'd been sure of that ever since John said she came highly recommended by a player…

Her whole life, she'd relied on him. First as her rock to see her through her mother's cancer and death, and then later to keep her safe and out of trouble when she went out to the clubs with her friend. He was always there. A few times, he'd even intercepted her from making a huge mistake and leaving with another guy.

At the time, she'd seen him as an overbearing friend of her brother's. Now, she saw his love for her had been a constant in her life, and she'd taken it for granted. Well, no more. First chance she got, she was going to fix their little problem and he wasn't going to stop her.

Night, G. Love U. She hurried and powered down her phone.

She had no desire to read his reply or wait to see if he'd give her more than a generic goodbye from a friend. She laid her head on the pillow and clutched her phone to her chest. Shauna and Dana's advice from earlier went through her thoughts. They were right. Professional athletes were a pain in the ass to handle, and impossible not to love.

Chapter Twenty-Six

A half an hour until game time, and Angie was nowhere to be found. Gary laced up his shoes. She wasn't picking up her phone, and she hadn't been at the hotel when he drove over there last night to check on her after reaching her voice mail all day long. For three long days, he'd had no idea what the fuck was going on.

He'd even had Drew call her to see if she'd answer his call, thinking she finally realized what he'd done and wanted no part of him. He struggled into the home jersey, not wanting to ask anyone for help. Truly alone, he wanted to get away from everyone. He wanted Angie.

"Hey, have you seen Angie? I'm supposed to warm up with her before the game." Lowry stood beside him, holding his uniform pants in his hand.

Gary shook his head. "Haven't seen her."

Lowry moved in closer. "Hey, man, is it true? Were you fucking around with her?"

Gary lunged for Lowry and smashed him against the locker, hands fisted in his shirt, face to face. "Don't go there."

"Jesus, Satchel, what the hell is wrong with you?" Pierce yanked the back of his jersey, but Gary refused to let go of Lowry.

"Don't even speak her name. Got it?" Gary gave him another shove before letting him go.

Pierce and Morgan pushed him behind the last row of lockers. Gary turned away from them and ran his hands through his hair. The last thing he needed was some asshole talking trash and getting Angie in more trouble.

"Want to tell us what went on back there for you to screw up before the first game of the season?" Morgan crossed his arms and put his foot on the bench in front of him.

"No." Gary glanced at them and punched the locker. "Just keep Lowry away from me, and tell him if he knows what's good for him, he won't open his damn mouth."

Morgan's brows rose. "He's not known for poppin' off before a game."

"Yeah, right." Gary shoulder shoved his way through Morgan and Pierce and turned. "Where's Coach?"

Pierce hitched his thumb over his shoulder. "Got called up into the main office with Doc and Angie."

"Fuck," Gary mumbled. "Thanks."

Tension and relief swept through him at the same time. He walked back to his locker and found Lowry gone. At least he knew where Angie was, and she hadn't done something stupid like take off for Deadhorse and walk away from her job. But a meeting before the game with the administrators? They'd let her go before the whistle blew to start the game.

The injustice of her punishment sucked. It was unfair to make her be the one responsible. He'd loved her for longer, and couldn't believe she'd fallen in love with him. Gary sat on the bench and stared at the tiled floor. Hell, that was his plan all along.

He'd talked himself into believing he was doing her a favor getting her a job with the Seahawks. Even told Drew he'd watch out for her and bring her back to Seattle and help her find a place to live. When all along, he hoped it was the right time, the right moment, the right conditions to come clean with how he felt about her.

He loved her.

There was never any doubt that she was the woman for him. He'd hidden the truth from Drew and everyone else, because he thought he was doing the best thing and staying away from her. The only person he was protecting was himself.

He was afraid of losing her. He had few little things in his life he'd loved. His mom, and she left him to the state. His friends, and he made sure to keep them close but they were ultimately just people in his life he didn't want to lose, with no real investment on his part. And then there was Angie.

For the longest time he tried to tell himself he'd built her up into the perfect woman, into someone he could keep at a distance without getting hurt. But now he knew everything about her: what she was like when she woke up in the morning, and how she needed someone to practically lie on top of through the night, so she could sleep. The reality of having her was more than even he expected.

He wasn't willing to lose her, no matter what.

If they fired her, he'd make up being an asshole toward her.

If they kept her on, he'd fight everyone to make sure they could have a relationship. If that included trading him to a different team, he'd gladly go.

"All right, listen up, team." Coach's voice boomed in the locker room.

Gary stood and turned around. His gaze found Angie first. She stood a few steps behind the coach with her shoulders back, her arms straight, and her eyes on Gary. His chest tightened. He'd expected a distraught Angie, and instead he found her strong, confident, and reassuring him with a single look.

"Lowry, Tanner, and Jenson, you'll see Doc for your warm up in the exercise room today," Coach said.

"What about Angie?" Lowry walked across the room.

"She's no longer employed…"

The voices buzzed in Gary's ears, but he ignored everything. Angie stepped around Coach and moved toward him, smiling. The moment she was close enough to touch, he hooked her neck and brought her against him.

He shook, having her back in his arms, half relieved their secret was over, and half angered over their relationship thrusting her back into unemployment.

"I'll speak with them," he whispered in Angie's ear.

She shook her head against his chest and then peered up at him. "You don't have to. I quit. They never brought up what happened between us. I asked for a meeting before the game today, because I didn't want to leave them in the lurch any more than I already am. They still have time to call in another massage therapist as my replacement for the rest of the season."

"What are you talking about?" He cupped her face. "You can't walk away."

"Yes, I can. I did. You talked about regrets, and the only one I'd ever have is if I picked a job over you." She inhaled deeply, and smiled. "You're the most important person in my life and I'm not willing to worry about a contract, or to hide how much I love you. You mean more to me than making money or having an awesome job on my résumé. Nothing else compares to coming home and loving you."

"Honey," he whispered, stroking her face. "I'm not worth that sacrifice."

"You're worth everything to me." Her toughness melted, and her gaze grew misty. "I won't let you lose me," she whispered back. "I love you."

He captured her mouth, and kissed her. No, he *kissed* her.

His hand came up and palmed the back of her head, holding her in place, and he showed her exactly what her promise meant to him. No one in his life ever put him first, made sure he was secure in knowing they were a permanent fixture in his life, and loved him more than anything else.

There were no words to describe what he was doing to her. His soul shattered and he wanted her to experience every emotion consuming him. She gave him everything back. His tongue tangled with hers. Her lips slipped into the perfect mold of his mouth. He held her still, wanting her to accept it all and she did without any question.

There was nothing but him and her. And the feelings.

When it was over and before she could speak, he said, "We're getting married."

"What?" She held on to him.

"After the game, we're flying to Vegas, and we're getting married. I'm not going another day without you." He kissed her quickly. "Call Drew and your dad if you want. Hell, call Jules, Grayson, and the rest of them and have them fly out too. But it's happening tonight."

Her lips broke out in a smile and her eyes lit up as she nodded her head. "We'll get married."

"Yeah." He laughed.

Cheers broke out in the room. His gaze snapped to the others. He'd forgotten they were even there. He pulled Angie back into his embrace and spoke to the team. "We're getting married tonight in Vegas. You're all invited."

Several minutes of congratulations, and Coach was bringing the team back to the game they were about to play. First game of the season, against the Raiders. Gary kissed Angie, and patted her ass as she walked away.

"Where are you going, Swanson?" Coach yelled.

Angie jolted and turned around. "Outside, Coach. I'm no longer part of the team and—"

"You're marrying Satchel, right?" Coach asked.

She nodded. "Yes, Coach."

"Then you're back on the team. We can't lose you if these men are going to stay healthy and off the bench," Coach hollered.

"Seriously?" Gary whispered, tightening his arm around Angie.

She glanced at Gary and back to the coach. "I get my job back?"

Coach ignored her question and focused his attention on Gary. "Can you keep your pants up while you're on Seahawk property?"

He bit down his grin and nodded. "Yes, Coach."

"Then shuttup and let's play some football tonight." Coach threw up his arms. "Get out there and kick ass. Make us one more game closer to the Super Bowl!"

Ten minutes later, Gary kissed Angie on the way down the tunnel to the field. "See you after the game."

"I'll be waiting." She swatted his ass. "Go win."

He jogged backward, not ready to look away from her yet, feeling truly alive for the first time in his life. "I already won."

She blew him a kiss. He turned and ran out into the field to the cheers of the fans. He glanced back at the tunnel and laughed. Angie, already bending the rules of her job, had followed him outside. Her fingers were in her mouth, and he swore he heard her whistle.

About the Author

Top selling romance author Debra Kayn lives with her family at the foot of the Bitterroot Mountains in beautiful Idaho. She enjoys riding motorcycles, playing tennis, fishing, and creating chaos for the men in the garage.

Her love of family ties and laughter makes her a natural to write heartwarming contemporary stories to the delight of her readers. Oh, let's cut to the chase. She loves to write about *REAL MEN* and the *WOMEN* who love them.

When Debra was nineteen years old, a man kissed her without introducing himself. When they finally came up for air, the first words out of his mouth were, "Will you have my babies?" Considering Debra's weakness for a sexy, badass man who is strong enough to survive her attitude, she said yes. A quick wedding at the House of Amour and four babies later, she's living her own unbelievable romance book.

More from This Author
(From *Conveniently* by Debra Kayn)

Dana hitched up her dress, dodged the groups of people milling around in the lobby of Timber Lodge, and ran for the long hallway. A crowd had gathered in hopes of catching a glimpse of one of the U.S. men's downhill skiers, but what they'd gotten instead was a front row seat to the most humiliating moment of Dana's life. Positive the laughter in the room was at her expense, she only wanted to escape.

Escape from the embarrassment of wearing a wedding dress with no groom, no wedding, and no idea what she was going to do now.

A figure stepped in front of her exit. She bumped into a man's unmovable chest. Stumbling to the side, she gazed up into a pair of dark eyes. Her barricade stared at her intently, while holding her arms to keep her from falling.

"S-sorry," she mumbled, pulling away from him as he attempted to keep her there.

She spotted an open door, ran, and slipped into the empty banquet room. She gazed at the vases filled with pastel pink flowers atop the tables, the unlit candles, and the ivory colored lace draped over every flat surface. Everything perfectly decorated for a quaint reception. The guests who were coming had quietly slipped away after her fiancé, Jace Kendall, announced he'd changed his mind about getting married, because he wasn't in love with her anymore.

She removed the diamond necklace from the jewelry box that Jace had thrust into her hands, to soften the fact he'd dumped her on her wedding day, before he'd hightailed his way out the door. "I'm going to annihilate him."

She tossed the box to the floor, dug her phone out of the clutch purse she'd bought specifically for her wedding day — while dropping the jewelry inside — and rang her father. "Daddy. I've got an emergency and need you to do something for me."

"What's going on? You sound upset," her dad said. "Weren't you scheduled to get married right now?"

A knock sounded on the outer door. She raised her gaze, ignored the rude person interrupting her, and continued. "Jace walked out on me, said he didn't love me the way a man loves a woman and … " she sniffed, "I want you to fire him. Kick him out of his office, and make sure someone else takes over his job."

"He's one of my best employees," her father said. "You'll get past this setback."

She squeezed her eyes closed and opened them again at the accusation in her dad's voice. "But, Daddy. *He* left *me*."

The door opened and a man decked out in skiwear entered. He stood staring at her, and she glared while continuing to talk on the phone. "No, I don't want you to fly here from Italy." She paused to listen. "No, I don't want you to fly me away to Barbados. I want to get *married*. I want to become Mrs. Somebody today. That's what's supposed to happen. At twenty-five years old, I'm supposed to get married. At twenty-eight, I'm having my first baby. It's my life schedule, Daddy. You know how I've planned all the important events in my life. Jace ruined everything."

Her father sighed, sounding at a loss. "Do you want to come back home? I can send Pete there to run the shop."

Dana's father would never understand her need for order. Too busy traveling with his fourth wife and Dana's three half-brothers, he'd even failed to find time to attend the wedding of his only daughter from his first marriage. She blew out her breath. "No! No, I'm sorry I bothered you … just go do whatever you're doing. I'll handle this myself. Bye, Daddy."

She disconnected the call and turned her attention to the man standing in the room with her. "What?"

"Are you okay?" He stepped forward, studying her in what appeared to be a mix of fascination and trepidation.

She grabbed her bodice and hitched her dress, squaring her shoulders. He acted as if he'd never seen a woman whose whole world had crumbled into a gazillion little pieces only moments ago. "I'm fine."

Dressed in a two-piece gray ski suit, with goggles sitting on the top of his head holding back shoulder-length black hair, he let his gaze take in the full length of her dress. His eyes, the color of mahogany, were heated and intense. A quiver traveled up her spine, not exactly unpleasant, but definitely unwanted. Right away, she pegged him for a player.

"If you're looking for the lobby, go out the door, turn right, and keep walking. You can't miss it. It's that huge room that's packed with everyone laughing and talking." She tapped her foot, itching to shed the dress and throw away anything that reminded her of Jace.

"I came here to check on you." He held his hands out to the sides of him. "I'm the guy you plowed into when you ran down the hallway. You looked like you were in trouble. I thought I'd see if I could help you with anything."

"There's nothing you can do for me except go." She kicked off her shoes and reached behind her, searching for the hidden zipper on the floor length, eggshell white gown she'd had specially made a year ago for this exact day. "You can leave and shut the door behind you."

He tilted his head. "You're shaking. Are you sure you're all right?"

"Yes, dammit." She grabbed her elbow and forced her other hand further down her back, trying to reach the tiny hook on her dress. "This is all Jace's fault."

"Who?"

She clamped her lips together and muffled her scream. Her eyes burned with unshed tears, and anger bubbled to the surface. She would not cry.

"What can I do?"

"Nothing," she snapped.

He tilted his head and his gaze dropped to her dress. "Babe … let me help. You're upset."

She studied him for a few blinks, turned around, and presented him with her back. "Fine. Undo my zipper for me, but hurry. I feel like I'm going to be sick, and I hate throwing up."

Her need to remove any remembrance of her planned marriage trumped any modesty she may have felt over standing in her underwear in front of a man she'd never met before. She wiggled her shoulders in impatience. "Please, hurry."

"I'll have you out of here in no time." His hand skimmed her back as he deftly undid her dress, including the eyehooks.

She shivered, blaming the chill on her emotions, and shimmied out of the wedding dress. The material pooled at her feet, and she was finally free from the suffocating dress that reminded her of everything she'd lost today. She glanced down at her body. The five-hundred dollar lingerie set that'd arrived yesterday from her stepmother was all wrong. There was nothing sacred or pure about her thoughts at the moment.

A low whistle reminded her she wasn't alone and the man wasn't leaving. She sighed in self-pity, because trouble seemed to keep jumping out and tripping her lately. She couldn't get a break.

Not in the mood to deal with another skier whose only goal was to screw every snow bunny that flooded the lodge this time of year, Dana tried to ignore him in hopes he'd go away. During the workweek, she had lots of practice pushing away the attention of men. Running the shop downstairs put her right in line to deal with every male in the lodge.

Except, as she paced the banquet room, she couldn't help glancing at the man who'd stayed to help her.

He was one of the sexiest skiers she'd seen visit the lodge. The long black hair hung haphazardly to his shoulders, the patch of whiskers under his lower lip accented full lips, and dark eyes surrounded with even darker lashes made him drool-worthy. Normally, his looks would've grabbed her attention.

If she didn't hate every single man on Earth at this moment.

She planted her hands on her bare hips. "You've had your fill. There's no more to see, so you can leave."

He seemed to gaze at her ivory colored lingerie with too much interest. She half turned. If he said one thing about the garter belt, the pantyhose, or her lack of clothing, she'd stab him with her four-inch Jimmy Choos.

He took a step toward her and stopped. "You're crying."

"I am not." She swiped her cheeks, upset to find wetness. She never cried. Not since she was twelve and broke her arm at Mount Shasta during ski camp.

He reached into the back pocket of his ski pants and extracted a handkerchief. She sniffed. Crying over Jace was a waste of good tears. She should be putting this energy into a backup plan.

"May I?" the skier whispered, motioning with the cloth, then stepping forward when she refused to answer and dotting her cheeks dry.

She gazed into his eyes and was surprised to find only concern. "What kind of man carries a handkerchief?"

"One that never knows if he'll meet a beautiful woman who'll need one." His gaze softened.

"Really?"

"No." His mouth curved upward. His perfect white teeth practically sparkled. "I use one to clean the moisture out of my goggles when I ski."

She wrinkled her nose. "Please tell me this doesn't have your sweat on it."

"Don't worry. I haven't hit the slopes yet."

"Oh." She dropped her gaze. "Well, thank you. That wasn't necessary, but it was … nice."

He hooked his thumb under her chin and lifted her gaze. "Will you be okay?"

The tenderness in his voice and the gentle touch undid her. She threw herself at him, burying her face in his neck, and sobbed.

She cried for her disappointing day, her pathetic wedding with no family and only the acquaintances from her father's business present to wish her well. Most of all she mourned for her failed life.

"Shh." He rubbed her back. "It can't be all bad."

Aware of the heat from the palm of his hand, Dana cried harder for her lost opportunity. She'd planned her life down to the most minuscule details in an effort to make sure she never ended up the way her parents had. Now it was over, and she had no idea what she was supposed to do next.

"Do you want to tell me what happened?" The man leaned back and held her by the upper arms, not letting her go.

"It doesn't matter. There's nothing I can do about it, not that I want to have that jerk back in my life." She blew her nose with the borrowed handkerchief. "Thanks for the shoulder and the h-handkerchief."

"My name's Juan."

"Dana." She inhaled a deep breath to compose herself. "I appreciate the help with the dress … and the hug. I'm okay now."

Juan frowned. She moistened her lips and tilted her head. He seemed familiar. Probably one of the men she'd sold equipment to, or passed by on her way downstairs in the lodge on her way to work over the last couple of months.

"Listen, I don't want to leave you while you're upset." He glanced around the room. "Why don't you put the dress back on, and I'll buy you a drink at the bar. It'll help you relax."

"Ugh." She walked over and sat atop a table pushed up against the wall. "I don't want to wear that *thing* ever again. I don't care if I have to walk up to my room wearing … " she raised her arms, "nothing. I refuse to have anything to do with Jace Kendall. Do you know him? Because I wouldn't be against you taking a bat to his car or decking him."

"No, I don't recognize the name." Juan cleared his throat. "You should forget about him. It sounds like you're better off with him out of your life."

"Yes, I am." But she didn't believe it. Jace had been the answer to her prayers for the last two years. "I suppose I better go up to my room."

"Dressed like that?" His brows rose.

"I'm not touching the wedding dress." She pointed to the floor where the yards and yards of expensive lace lay discarded. "Besides, I'm hideous."

"You're lovely, and I don't think walking out there into the lodge is wise considering the place is filled to capacity with men desperate to look at a beautiful woman."

"I doubt that." She shrugged. "Don't you think if men were willing to be with me, I would've gotten married today instead of being dumped at the front door?"

Juan winced. "He's a fool."

"He didn't even wait until we stepped in front of the minister before he chickened out. He screwed up my whole life. If I don't get married today, I'll never be able to reach my next goal."

He made a sympathetic noise.

"Not only that, Now I'm probably never going to experience what it's like to have a hon — " She clamped her lips together, then mumbled, "Never mind."

Juan shrugged off his coat, walked over, and sat beside her. She shook her head, unwilling to believe she was sitting here, when she should be slipping upstairs to enjoy her honeymoon. Jace could rot in hell for all she cared.

"Here. Cover up. You're shaking." Juan slipped his coat over her shoulders. "I've already missed most of my slope time. You can borrow my coat."

She pushed the sleeves of the coat to her wrists, noticing it was one of her daddy's products. "Thanks. I'm sure I won't be the only woman caught running up the back stairs in her panties. I run into at least one woman a week sneaking out of the rooms the Olympic team uses."

"Is that so?" He unzipped his pants. "You can wear these too, I have spandex underneath. It'll be safer. No one looks at a man half undressed going up the back stairs."

"I don't know why you're being so nice to me." Dana sighed. "But I do appreciate it. I'm not the spoiled brat Jace said I was. He was just … "

"An asshole?" He cussed, struggling with his zipper.

"Yes. Incredibly stupid and egotistical too." She glanced down at the front of his pants. "What's wrong?"

"Damn thing's stuck."

She pushed his hands aside. "It's the zipper. Happens all the time. Metal zippers rust over time, especially when subjected to the moist, cold weather the clothing is intended for … big mistake. That's why Reese Enterprise uses plastic or coated zippers in all outerwear clothing."

"Huh?" His hands stilled and he glanced at her.

"It's not important." She pushed his hands away. "Here, I'll help."

"We need a pair of scissors." He peered down at the front of him. "Or maybe you can rip it."

She tugged, but it only drew the zipper tighter, making it catch more. Without anything to use, she leaned over and opened her mouth.

"Whoa … " Juan sank his hands into the hair piled on the top of her head. "I'd like nothing more, but having your mouth on me when you're upset probably isn't the smartest decision."

She paused with her opened mouth above the zipper and gazed up at him. "You don't want me to try and bite the string in half?"

He chuckled and patted her head before removing his hand and leaning back. "Be careful with those teeth, babe."

She lowered her head, caught the edge of the material, and ground her teeth back and forth. It was harder than she'd imagined. She grunted and worked the string over to her eyetooth.

The zipper grew taut and she reached up and tugged at the material. She stilled with her hand against his crotch. There was a reason for the lack of space between the fabric and the man. A very big reason.

Warmth flooded her face. Her skin tingled. The bulge underneath the pants fascinated, yet shocked her. A heady sensation, considering she could almost feel the heat radiating off him on her cheek.

The door opened and a flash went off in the room. She frowned at the same time the string gave way and she jerked away from Juan, spitting the remains of the thread off her lip. She stood and glanced behind her.

A robust, angry man in a coat with the USA Olympics emblem scrolled across the chest stood inside the doorway. Two photographers snapped pictures behind him, blinding Dana from inspecting them any further. Juan jumped off the table and stepped in front of her, blocking her from view.

"Oh, shit," Juan muttered.

"What are they doing?" she whispered, zipping Juan's coat to her neck. She wasn't sure if that helped, because on the bottom half, she still wore her thong and garter. "Who are they?"

Juan straightened, keeping his hand on her hip to keep her hidden behind his body. "It's not what it looked like, Coach Lindhurst."

"It was exactly what it looked like, and it'll be on the front cover of *Sports Illustrated* in the morning thanks to your carelessness. You were supposed to meet with the press a half-hour ago. Looks like that won't be necessary. They've got their pictures, and I imagine more than an article or two to fill the damn magazine, thanks to you and your entourage." Coach Lindhurst growled. "I've warned you. Your sponsor warned you. One more scandal and your benefactors would pull their money. I'm going to have to put you on reserve, dammit. You've really screwed up this time, Santiago."

Juan stepped forward, stopped, and glanced back at Dana. He gave her a hint of a smile before turning around. "Yes, Coach. If I could request another meeting, I can explain what happened here. It's a simple misunderstanding. One that shows that the lady behind me is innocent, and shouldn't be involved with any gossip that comes my way. She's had a bad day, sir."

Coach Lindhurst shook his head in disgust. "You had one more month to return and win another gold, and you threw it away because of some woman who wants a piece of — "

"Stop. Seriously, don't go there, or we're going to have problems between us. I'll talk to Wyden. I'll get my sponsor back," Juan said. "Can you keep me on the roster until then?"

"It's out of my hands. You had two warnings. Three marks and you're out. Balden will go in your place. You're immediately on reserve." Coach stared Juan down, cursed, and headed toward the door.

She scrambled out from behind Juan. "Wait!"

"What are you doing?" Juan whispered.

She ignored him, stepped over, and picked up her wedding dress, holding it in front of her. "Juan's right. There's a simple explanation for what you saw. You see, we're getting married. He was helping me into my dress, and I was helping him out of his suit. You can go to the lobby. There's a minister waiting for us. We're already late though, so if you'll excuse us, we need to finish getting dressed."

Juan walked over and ushered everyone out of the room, a look of bemusement on his face. Dana crossed her arms and cradled her elbows in her hand. It didn't take a genius to figure out Juan was on the Olympic team, and he was in deep trouble. She owed him for being so kind to her.

The more she thought about actually marrying him, the better she felt. She'd stay on her schedule, and figure out what to do later when she had time to think over her rash decision. She'd prove to Jace and her father that she was not spoiled. She'd help Juan for the goodness of the United States.

"Thanks, babe, but I can take it from here. This is my fault and I only have myself to blame." Juan ran his hands through his hair and groaned. "I'll figure out some way to make it back on the team with a new sponsor. This isn't the first time I've had to go in front of the board and prove myself to them."

She took off his coat and pushed it into his chest. "Get dressed."

"What?" He slipped his arms in the sleeves. "I said you could take the jacket. I've got plenty."

"We'll have to hurry or the minister will leave." She stepped into her dress and turned around. "Zip me up."

"You're not serious?"

She patted her hair. "I take it you need an excuse for what that man saw in here today to get back on the Olympic team, and I have a deadline. We're getting married."

"We can't." He tilted his head and looked up at the ceiling. "This is not happening to me."

"Yes, it is." She grabbed his hand. "I'm Dana Reese. My daddy is Colton Reese of Reese Enterprise. You know, the owner of the most popular line of ski equipment. He'll sponsor you, and be happy you took me off his hands. Trust me."

"Are you serious?"

"More than you'll ever know. I won't let Daddy or Jace ruin my life schedule." She laughed hysterically. "Let's go get married."

And check out these Debra Kayn Crimson Romance titles:

Seductively

Wildly

Breathing His Air

In the mood for more Crimson Romance?
Check out *The Look-Alike Bride* by Kathryn Brocato at
CrimsonRomance.com.

www.ingramcontent.com/pod-product-compliance
Lightning Source LLC
Chambersburg PA
CBHW011934050726
47590CB00011B/3290